THE BOY WHO SLEPT WITH BEARS

By
George R. Douthit, III

RHYOLITE PRESS, LLC

Published in the United States of America by Rhyolite Press, LLC
P.O. Box 2406
Colorado Springs, Colorado 80901
www.rhyolitepress.com

The Boy Who Slept with Bears / George R. Douthit, III
First Printing 2004
Second Printing 2005

This work was originally published in slightly different form by Juniper Press, Inc. in 2004. This revised and expanded edition is published by arrangement with the author.

Library of Congress Control Number: 2013944362
ISBN 978-0-9839952-8-9

Cover design and book design/layout by Donald R. Kallaus

Author photo, © 2013, Donald R. Kallaus

"A recorder of what has been done is equal to the greatest hunter, the bravest warrior, or even the holy man." he said. "To be such a historian, such a recorder, you must learn to see all things, know how they look, and how they are done. You must see that the young colt swims on the downstream side of the mother, behind the wall of her body, and that the wind does not always push the arrows of the just. As the hills of one's youth are all mountains, and the hunts all seem fat after the meat is long eaten, so memory makes every man the bravest in his long-ago encounters, and the enemies faced in battle become very many as the warrior days retreat. The picture is the rope that ties memory solidly to the stake of truth."

Picture Maker,
a member of the Sioux Nation
from **The Story Catcher**, by Marie Sandoz

DEDICATION

To my grandfather Charlie Beck, my "old man" who let me wade bare legged in Skunk Creek, one hot day in 1936, in South Dakota; and to my wonderful wife, Alice Irene, and the greatest family a man could have. A special thanks of course, to Jim Ciletti and members of my writers critique group who greatly enhanced this little journey.

CHAPTER 1

March 18, 1880
Southern Ute Reservation
Ignacio, Colorado

I bolted straight up when a tent flap on our lodge cracked in the dark like the sound of the white soldier's revolver. Trembling, I pulled my buffalo robe about my shoulders and stared into the shadows of our tepee. I did not know where I was until I saw Grandfather's war shield hanging in the firelight. Wind roared like Kwiakati, the grizzly bear, when he is angry. It was the time of miwipi kacuai, when buckskin was boiled into soup, and we went to our robes each night with empty bellies.

"What is it, Tomas?" Mother whispered sharply from beneath her robe.

"A dream," I mumbled. "A dream." Mother rolled back to sleep. My grandfather, Cloud Whiskers, snored.

I rubbed my eyes, looking to the place where my father, Chavas, should have slept. Blue coats killed him while he was hunting in the month when everything turns yellow. This was during the time the agent Meeker and his farmhands were killed and our angry cousins took the agency women captive along the Smoking Earth River in the north.

My name is Sak-wa-ma-tu-ta-ci, meaning "Blue Hummingbird." My mother gave me this name at my birth thirteen winters past. But my name was taken from me by the strange white agent Jabez Craven, who could not say many Ute words. He called me Tomas—Tomas Dequine, the name Dequine from the family of my Mexican mother, Ursilita Dequine. We were members of Sopata's band of Capotes—Southern Utes—herded like the white man's cows by soldiers from New Mexico to this small place in Colorado—all that is now left of our land among the Shining Mountains.

I think it is wrong that a man can take away the name of another, or tell him where he may live—or kill his father while that man is only hunting.

Outside our tent the wind screamed and the heavy elk-hide sides were sucked in and out like a buffalo dying from the hunter's lance. As I stared into the few remaining embers of our warming fire, my mind began to clear of sleep, and hunger returned to gnaw like Kaci-ci, the rat. Hunger was with us always this winter, for we were not allowed to leave the reservation to hunt, and there was little game to be found here. Snows came early in the high country. We had been told the rations promised by Washington as payment for our taken lands were being held on the far side of the mountains in the white camp called Alamosa. They would remain there until the road over the pass was open.

My hunger was made greater by the smell from the piñon smoke and the wild sage gathered two days ago by Mother and Aunt Kanav. For many nights, all of The People have gone to their lodges with only dreams of food. Jonejo and Peoch and others have cut up their rawhide parfleches, pouches in which they store their belongings, and boiled the leather for soup. If it had not been for the broth that Mother made from the bark of the cottonwood tree, Grandfather and I would have gone to bed with nothing.

The drumbeats, cries, and songs of Azumpitz, our shaman,

sounded above the winds. The forlorn shrieking sounds came from Pazio's lodge across the creek where his old woman lay dying from the cold and hunger. My own stomach hurt from the emptiness. I did not want to die, and I was ashamed of my fear.

As I lay in my robe, I thought much of hot buffalo hump, with the juices running down my arm, browning venison ribs, and beaver tail roasting in the flames of our campfire, the grease hissing and spattering into the coals. I wanted to be in the south again, along the Rio San Juan in New Mexico, where we were warm, where we had much to eat—before my father was killed. Dawn, an Apache girl with the large eyes, long black hair, and a voice like the lark taught me new songs. She showed me how to draw with charcoal from the campfires. I think of her often and dream of playing the flute for her one day when I have become a man and a maker of pictures. Wind rattled the dewclaws tied to the smoke ears on the top of our lodge. The sounds became one with the cries of Azumpitz as I lay back, burrowing deeper beneath my robe, and slept.

In the morning, I opened my eyes to a great commotion.

"Out. Out of here!" Grandfather Cloud Whiskers sat upright, shouting and flailing his long thin arms at a black crow flapping wildly in our tent. The bird escaped through the smoke hole. "It flew into my face two times." Grandfather complained.

"This is a bad sign." He drew a blanket about his shoulders, pushing himself to stand, stamping the cold from his feet and legs. "There will be more trouble." Grandfather believed in many of the old ways.

"Tomas," Mother whispered. There was urgency in her voice but a small laughter in her eyes. "Get up. Go and get a burning stick from your aunt Kanav. Our warming fire is out."

"May Pagits come back with me, Mother?"

"Yes. Tell your aunt that I have found enough corn to make shaguie."

The piñon, yucca, and cactus were white with frost. In the east, icy skies burning with the fire of the rising sun were reflected on the snowy mountaintops. There were few camp sounds this morning. Smoke rose from the lodges. Dogs huddled near tents as I made my way along the short trail to Aunt Kanav's lodge. Uncle Porache, husband of Kanav and father of my cousin Pagits, was killed by the Arapaho four years ago when The People went to hunt buffalo on the plains east of Denver. Father looked after my aunt and cousin. Now, I have tried to help them. Pagits was younger and not as tall as I. I shook my cousin in his robe.

"Go away," Pagits grumbled.

"You sleep like the bear in its winter den. Get up. Hot shaguie is waiting for us at our lodge. Get up or I will eat it all."

Pagits scrambled to put on his moccasins and wrap himself in his blanket. Before slipping outside he grabbed at my arm. "The truth, Tomas?"

"The truth," I replied. "Hot shaguie and Mother needs a fire stick."

"You work great magic, Tomas," Aunt Kanav said, smiling. "Go before this fire stick is cold." She handed me the burning stick.

On our way we passed the place where Pazio's tent should have been, but was gone—taken down. His piwan had died in the night. Her clothing lay piled on the ground, for it was the custom to give away the belongings of one who has gone to the spirit world. Some of our women stood wailing in the cold. They had cut off their hair to mourn the passing of this good woman. I turned away as I remembered the times this grandmother had given Pagits and me fried bread and honey.

"Are you afraid to die, Tomas?" Pagits asked.

"No. We are not going to die, Cousin," I told him. I wanted to be gone from this place where the spirits of the dead lingered.

"Have you ever seen a ghost?" Pagits asked.

"Many times, little cousin." I grabbed his arm and pulled him along. "Now, let us go from here." We returned to our lodge.

"Did you boys lose your way?" Mother asked. Gently she pulled Pagits's braid, taking the fire stick from my hand. She knelt upon the ground, then placed the glowing end of the stick against a small pile of bark and twigs. She blew on it, and soon a warm fire burned.

Squatting to warm my hands, I told Mother, "Pazio's woman is dead."

"He has taken his carniva down," Pagits added in a whisper. "Tomas saw her ghost. Will we all die, Aunt?"

"Shush, Pagits. Don't talk of ghosts. If you two die it will be because old Siaci the witch has caught you. Go now, and wash in the creek or I will boil a stone for your breakfast." She pinched my cheeks. "You are both like Kwiakati, who sleeps the winter away with enough fat upon his bones to live until spring." Looking back, I saw on her face and in her eyes a sadness for Pazio's woman.

Grandfather sat on a log warming his body against the fire. He complained again of the bird that had flown into our carniva that morning. "It is a bad omen when a blackbird flies into a man's lodge." He held one hand in the other and massaged the stiffness from his fingers. Mother served him shaguie made from roasted corn and the milk of our old goat. If an elder is not served first, my mother might grow old before her time.

"When you are through, you can take what is left to your mother, Pagits." She poured out cereal for my cousin and me. For one who has fought the Navajo and Arapaho—even the Sioux along the Platte River—I thought my grandfather showed great worry over a blackbird.

"If we do not find game soon, Grandfather, we may have to hunt and eat your blackbird," I said, smiling at Pagits. Mother scowled at me.

"Heh," the old man growled. "In my day one did not make light of a bird inside one's lodge. I have seen great misfortune come about because of this."

Pagits and I turned our faces away to keep from laughing. We were too late.

"You boys think this is a thing to laugh about, eh? Washington will make good farmers out of you both. Things have changed since I was a boy."

"We did not mean to laugh, Grandfather," I told him.

Mother looked at us sternly, then back to the old man. She said, "We must have game soon, Grandfather, or we will starve." She bent to the fire, removed a blackened coffeepot from the embers, and poured coffee into tin cups for us. Grandfather wrapped his hands about the heated cup as he held it.

"I remember a place two sleeps from here," I said. "A stream in a valley surrounded on both sides by hills. It is like a dream." I turned to my grandfather. "You and Father took me there when I was a small boy. There were deer and elk and beaver. There were fish in the beaver dams and wild ducks in the ponds."

"This place you speak of is part of the land that has been sold to the whites for their cattle, is it not?" Mother asked.

Grandfather slurped his coffee loudly. "Sold and not paid for. The way of Washington. Taken from us, I would say." He slammed his empty cup down on the log. "No man has a right to sell the land to another," he said. "The land belongs to no one."

"We might go there one night in the dark," I said.

"Since the killings of that agent and the murder of your own father by the soldiers in the north, there is no way to leave this place, not even in the dark, " Grandfather said. "The blue coats would come after us as they have in the past, and I am too old to fight or run anymore."

"If you were to go and see Craven, Grandfather, we would not have to run or fight. I believe he would let us leave if we promised to return." Steam from my words dissolved into the cold air like smoke.

"Hah. What does a boy who makes fun of a blackbird in a man's tent know of these things? That agent does not care if all of The People starve," Grandfather said. "There is much wrong with him. He hides his eyes behind the white man's eyeglasses that are the color of grass. He has a beaver hat, as do the men from Washington, that he never takes off. I believe it is stuck to his head. I have heard from Azumpitz that he drinks whiskey—has dreams in which he is pursued by bad spirits. He screams with anger—falling to the floor as a mad dog. Our elders and some of the young men have complained to the government about him. We hope he will be sent away."

"Would it not be dangerous, even with his permission, to leave at this time?" Mother asked.

"I would not be afraid," I said.

"Bravery is more than dancing with skinny Apache girls, or wandering the woods in the rain and drawing on rocks, Tomas," Grandfather said. He looked at Mother. "Did you know your son walks in the rain, Daughter? I have heard he even talks with the birds and animals."

Mother moved behind me, led me to sit, and began to brush my hair with her porcupine brush. She wove it into braids, as she had Father's. "You are too young for girls," she said. "I do not know about the wandering and the standing in the rain. Hold still, Tomas." She boxed my head softly. "It is not right that we must ask another where we may hunt," Mother said. "Perhaps we should have gone to live near our cousins in the north before the killings, where there was much game."

"Even though there was game there, Daughter," Grandfather said, "there were other hungers. Jorgenson the blacksmith tells me the agent Meeker made The People live in the square houses of the whites—plowed up their racetrack and the green meadows. He threatened to shoot their horses." Grandfather's brown eyes drilled into the fire. "It is no wonder he and his hands were killed. A man can stand only so much."

Mother finished braiding my hair. She carefully wrapped the ends of each braid in otter skin, then dropped the braids back to fall upon my chest. When she was through, she took my hands and held them, looking at me. I saw my own brown eyes and features in her face. Her cheeks were wrinkled from the sun and wind of many winters. She spoke. "Perhaps wandering in the rain is not a bad thing." There were tears in her eyes. "How often I brushed your father's hair," she said.

I would rather face the grizzly bear, than Craven, I thought. I would not go see him. I would rather starve. Grandfather must go to see the agent.

CHAPTER 2

March 21, 1880
Southern Ute Reservation
Ignacio, Colorado

On a morning after three sleeps had passed, Grandfather came from washing at the creek. With ice water dripping from his hair, he bent down to the fire. "I have had a dream, Grandson," he said. Mother filled our cups with the last of our coffee. "In this dream," he continued, "you went to see the agent Craven and you asked him if we might go away from this place to hunt, and he gladly gave you his permission." Grandfather looked away from me, a small grin on his face.

Mother stared at him. "Are you certain of this?"

I did not think Grandfather's eyes believed his words. With a finger at his lip, he appeared thoughtful. "It may not have been a dream, for as you know, Daughter, when one tosses in his sleep from hunger, it is difficult to be certain in the morning if one is thinking or dreaming."

Mother turned away to become busy carrying our sleeping robes from the tepee and hanging them over a frame to air. The meeting with Craven and the plan to go away and hunt had been discussed at a council the day before. Grandfather and I were chosen to speak for our band. Neither of us was anxious to face the agent, for Craven had great powers given to him by the white God and the soldiers in Washington. There was also the matter of the whiskey. The People did not like him.

Not to offend him again, I chose my words with care. "I have heard often of your bravery, Grandfather. You fought the Cheyenne and the Arapaho and rode with the soldiers against the Navajo. You chased the Sioux near the river the whites call Platte. With this bravery it would be proper for you to speak with Craven to save our lives," I said.

He replied, "That is true, Tomas, but my son, Chavas, your father, was a respected leader, and as his son you have a right—even an obligation—to go and ask this thing of the agent. Craven is not like the bear. He will not bite you. Take your cousin with you. When he sees how thin you both have become he will feel sorry for you."

"But I am—"

Grandfather went to relieve himself.

Mother returned. "Craven and your grandfather are like the coyote and the badger," she whispered to me. "When they meet on a single path there is a gnashing of teeth, growling, and in the end, fur flies. It is your duty to respect your grandfather's words." I would go and see the agent. If one of us did not, there would be more hardship and death for others of our band.

The following morning, I dressed in my new beaded leggings and a yellow overshirt Mother made from cloth sent by Washington the year before. I had a new blanket from our trade with the Navajo. "Do I look well?" I asked.

"You do not have to dance with Craven," Grandfather said.

Mother went into our carniva and returned, carrying a long deer-hide parfleche. She untied the thongs and rolled it out. It contained my father's flute, his lance, his bow, and a few arrows. From a smaller hide bag, she pulled out the silver peace medal given to my father at Taos by the white scout Carson, and a silver armband with a crude figure of a grizzly bear scratched on its surface. My father, too, had worn this band. Quinch, the Apache who was with Father when he was killed, had returned it to my mother. I remembered the peace medal. Father wore it only on special occasions, such as Bear Dance, or at meetings with men from Washington. Mother held up the bracelet.

"This bracelet came into the possession of our family before your grandfather was born, even before his grandfather was born, when the Ute and the Comanche fought together against the Spanish. It was during the time the first black robes came to this land from across the water to tell The People of the white God's son who was nailed to the wood cross. The bracelet has been given to the eldest son since that time and has much power. Your father wore it, and now it is yours to wear during your lifetime. You are also to have his medal from Washington." Mother took my hand and placed the bracelet upon my arm. It hung loosely, slipping back to my wrist.

"I will wear this bracelet about my wrist until it will stay upon my arm," I said. "I believe you should wear his peace medal, Mother." I placed it around her neck and brushed my lips across her cheek.

"Your son is too thin," Grandfather said. "If we are allowed to leave and hunt, we might be able to fatten him up with elk liver and beaver tail."

Mother grinned at Grandfather and me. "Your grandson is thin yet, but he is as handsome as his father was. And his grandfather still is," she added. "Tomas, I have been saving the lance and bow and arrows for you, and I know your father would have wanted you to have them. I will wear the medal until you are older."

I held her hands in mine, and then picked up the items. Why? I asked myself. If this silver band had power, how could the white man's gun have killed my father? I was pleased to have his lance and flute and bow. I would fetch Pagits and we would go and see if this Craven could dance.

On the way to see the agent, Pagits was frightened. "I do not like this," he said. "Craven sends boys and girls to the school at Grand Junction. Some are not heard from again."

"That's true," I said. "Porache and his sister went to the Indian school and became ill and died. Others have gone blind."

"Their hair is cut off and they are made to wear strange clothes," Pagits said. "They must talk as the Maricats—punished if they speak in the old language of The People."

"Speak no more of this school, Pagits," I said.

Would I see my mother again—and grandfather—or would Craven beat my cousin and me as stray animals? Would our hair be cut off? It was said this happened to Indian children in the white schools. What if the agent should cut off our ears with his sword, as Uncle Kiko said happened once to a Muache boy who would not mind a white solder? "That boy was forever known as No Ears," Uncle told me.

"Do not make Craven angry," I warned my cousin. "You are only a boy. I am almost a man. I will speak. You must remain silent. Maricats do not like noisy children."

"I will be happy to wait outside for you, Tomas."

"No. You must come inside with me, Cousin."

A blue coat stood guard in front of the agency building. He eyed us as if we should not have been there, then motioned us inside. The agent's office contained chairs, a desk, a table, wall maps, and oil lamps. A fire burned in a tall iron stove. Two blue coats sat in chairs tipped back against the wall. Pagits stood back waiting inside by the door. Craven sat at the table scratching a pen on papers.

Currie, the army doctor with hair like fire, stood beside

Craven, looking over the agent's shoulder. The People called the doctor Red Hair. A large, bearded white man I did not know leaned on the edge of the table facing the agent. When Pagits and I entered the room, this man turned to stare into my face, and I saw he had eyes and long hair the color of gray winter skies. He did not smile.

I waited. The stranger turned back to Craven. He slammed his large open palm on the table, muttering words to the agent through teeth clamped shut. He turned again and stalked with heavy steps from the agent's office, glaring at me before slamming the door behind him. The blue coats grinned at one another. I wanted to leave, but Craven had seen me.

I edged toward the table, and Red Hair raised his head to nod at me. We liked Currie. He was a friend. We did not trust Craven. He wore a tall hat, and I could not see his eyes behind the glasses. His mustache and beard were the color of the fox's tail. They nearly covered his face. One could not see much of his face. The People thought him a strange, distant man, wanting only to tell us of the white man's God. When we danced or played our drums, this one would lock the doors to the agency building and hide inside unless he had been drinking whiskey. Then he would come out and holler at us and sing church songs and scold us. He lived without a woman.

Grandfather said the agent was like a man he knew who lived with his mother and was half woman.

The agent looked up over his glasses.

Red Hair interpreted our words for us.

"What is it?" The agent grumbled.

I could not speak.

The agent spoke again in a louder voice. "What is it that you want?"

"I am Tomas Dequine, the son of Chavas, grandson of Cloud,

a—Cloud Whiskers," I stammered.

"I know who you are, Tomas Dequine, and I certainly know your grandfather." Craven twisted the tip of his mustache with thumb and finger.

"Craven," I said. I saw no sword.

"Speak up, boy." The agent squawked loudly as he spoke. "As you can see, we have been quite busy attempting to pacify this miner who says he has been harassed by your people. I am sick to death of the Indians' behavior and all the trouble it causes with the ranchers and miners."

I placed my hand over the bracelet, hoping its power would allow me to explain our needs as well as I could. "I do not know about that miner," I said. "I am here because we are hungry, Pazio's wife has died, and some are ill. In the lodge of my grandfather, there is nothing left to eat, only goat's milk. We have no game to hunt in this place. Our rations have not come from Washington." I breathed deeply as if I had run a long way. I continued. "There is a place not far called Beaver Creek. We believe there is game there. We are here to ask the agent for his permission to go there and hunt. We will return before the month of Leaves Coming."

Craven cocked his head slowly like the crane. When he spoke, his voice was sweet like a grandmother's. "Why aren't you away at school, young man?"

My heart beat like a war drum.

"We will deal with that later. Now, I knew your father, Craven said. "I replaced your name Sakam—whatever it was—with a good American name. I certainly know your disagreeable grandfather. I also know that your people are hungry. However, since your relatives in the north murdered poor Mr. Meeker and his people, and abducted the women, I can't have you running all over the country hunting and scaring the settlers and prospectors to death. You must learn to be patient."

Pagits giggled from the back of the room.

Craven frowned. "If I allow one of you to go off the reservation, I will have to allow all of you. Can you imagine what a problem this would be for Washington? I cannot keep track of you all now. We have been attempting to count the number of your people residing here. When I ask them their name they reply, "No name." This behavior is absurd and must stop. You are like a swarm of bees. Certainly you all have names." He leaned forward and I smelled his breath. It was a sweet scent of sour grapes.

"Bees?" I said.

"Bees!" Craven shouted, waving his arms and flitting his fingers about. "Wild bees. Honey bees. Here, there, everywhere."

"He doesn't understand why you call his people bees," Currie said. He attempted to translate the agent's words for me, adding a buzzing sound.

"Oh, yes," I laughed loudly. "Bees." I waved my own fingers in the agent's face.

"And another thing, Tomas Dequine," Craven continued. "Despite my unending labors, your people continue to impede the advancement of their civilization by not washing or changing clothing, although I must admit their barbarous custom of painting and cloaking themselves with feathers and animal hides is not as prevalent as it was when I came here. God does not want us to wear feathers in our hair, but he does want us to be clean, boy." The agent lowered his voice, smiling sweetly, and stroked his chin whiskers again. "That is the beauty of attending school, getting a white education."

"I will speak of your words, Craven, to Grandfather and my friends—that they must wash more and change clothes." My hands tightened into fists as the words of the agent I did not fully understand flowed. I had failed in my mission—but I would not leave. Where was the power in this bracelet?

Craven stood and walked a crooked path to the stove, where he turned to warm his thin backside and nearly leaned against the iron stove. The captain followed the agent, spoke to him quietly, and both men returned. Craven sat again. "Captain Currie makes an excellent point. If you and your people were to bring back enough meat for all, it would save Washington money." He nodded slowly. "I will allow you, your family, and several others to leave the reserve for three weeks. Take Topotsuk, Quinch—even your grandfather—and those men who are strong enough to make the trip and who you know are good hunters. You will need women with you to prepare the game, I am sure."

Craven wrote on a sheet of paper and passed it to the captain, who made his mark also. I placed the paper in my pocket. Father's bracelet did have power.

Craven went on. "You must be aware there are dangers off the reserve even greater than hunger," Craven said. The agent glanced at Currie. "A Ute Indian was recently hung by ranchers near Gunnison for stealing cattle. Your own Chief Ouray has said that you must not steal from the settlers or threaten the gold miners. I have signed a paper saying that you are good Indians—that you mean no harm. You must carry this paper at all times. Now go, and we will see about sending you to school when you return."

As we left the agent's office, I waved the paper at Pagits. "You see, Cousin, Grandfather was wrong. That blackbird in our tent has brought us only good fortune. And this medicine is strong." I held up my arm and spun the bracelet around my wrist. Perhaps I will stay in the mountains where there is game, I thought. Where there are no agents, where there are no white schools.

CHAPTER 3

March 24, 1880
Southern Ute Agency
Ignacio, Colorado

Permission to leave the reservation to hunt gave many of The People a sense of hope. One could see it in their eyes, hear it in their voices for the first time in many moons. Also, we learned from the blacksmith that the agent Craven would be replaced. There were several of our best hunters and a few of our women willing and strong enough yet to make the journey to the valley where we would hunt. Among these were Grandfather, Mother, Aunt Kanav, Pagits, Uncle Kiko, Quinch the Apache, and Topotsuk. We left as soon as preparations were made.

In three sleeps we arrived at our destination, finding that snow remained within the shadows of the pine on the north slopes of hills bordering the stream. Melting snows fed the creek and formed shallow puddles on the greening meadows where ducks shot like arrows into the skies. Red-winged blackbirds rose from greening willows like puffs of pipe smoke. There were wild turkeys. Quinch killed a deer, and our bellies were full for the first time in many moons.

The women followed on their own mounts, the animals dragging the travois upon which were carried our hide tepees and parfleches filled with the supplies for camp. My mother and others laughed, even sang. Life was good again.

Two of Uncle Kiko's favorite hunting dogs dragged along, noses to the ground, breaking to chase birds and once cornering a porcupine in a tree. Kiko scolded them. "Come here dogs or I will be pulling needles from your worthless hides." The dogs nosed about a tumble of lichen-stained aspen and pine carried down the slopes by a winter avalanche. They growled, and the hair on their backs stood. They did not want to leave that place.

"There is a bad spirit here," Quinch said.

"A smell of death," Topotsuk said.

"Perhaps a deer or bear caught in the falling of the rocks," Grandfather said.

I felt a chill and was glad when we rode on. As I turned away, I had the sense that I had seen movement far above at the edge of the woods. My concerns were forgotten, however, when Uncle Kiko directed us to the willow-lined banks of the stream where beaver ponds held trout.

"I believe we should have fresh fish for our supper," Mother said.

"A fine idea," Kiko said. "I will show these young men how to catch fish."

"You must first know yourself, my friend," Grandfather shouted. "You and Pagits must stay away from the water," the old man continued, frowning, shaking a thin finger at my cousin and me. "Pa Ah Pache will drag you both into the water and drown you."

Pagits's eyes grew wide. Pa Ah Pache was a spirit that lived in the water, snatching children if they came too close. I was not a child now. I was a man—not afraid even of Craven or that miner. I was not afraid of the water spirit. I would catch many fish. As we hurried our horses along, the men spoke excitedly of deer and elk killed here in years past—until our way was suddenly halted by a fence made from lodgepole pine running from the streambed all across the meadow and up into the hills bordering one side of the valley.

"Why do men build fences?" Pagits asked.

"To hold their cattle. To keep others from the land. It is the way of the Maricats. There will be many fences soon," Cloud Whiskers replied.

"One will not be able to ride a good horse far from his lodge," Quinch said. "It comes from giving away the land."

"I will show you what I think of this fence." I shouted, startling even myself, as I rode to the fence leaning the rear end of my horse against it. The poles gave way easily, tumbling to the ground. "So much for that fence," I yelled, with loud approval coming from most of our party we passed through the opening. Grandfather did not look pleased.

"In that place ahead there are aspen and pine for shelter," Kiko said. "This is where we once killed a large elk."

Cloud Whiskers replied, "You are losing your memory, Kiko. It was farther up the way." Then Grandfather's face became serious again. "This fence is a bad thing. I do not like it."

I was grateful when we reached the campsite. The women began to unpack the parfleches, erect the tepees, and build a fire. We men returned to the beaver dams to catch fish. There was great excitement when we found the day-old tracks of a large grizzly bear in the mud.

"We must be wary of this one," Topotsuk said.

We dammed a narrow branch of the stream with brush and stones to form a small pond. Pagits and I waded into the stream above the pond and drove the trout to the pool where we caught several of them by hand. The men—even Grandfather—were like children: splashing and falling down into the cold water, laughing and shouting.

Suddenly, my feet and legs were seized—drawn down by something from below. I was entangled in a quagmire of soft sucking mud and willow roots. I screamed. "Help me! Pa Ah Pache has me!" I felt wiry, scaly fingers holding me, and I fell backward into the mud and stream, my head underwater, to be drowned like the beaver in a trap. I was rescued from certain death by Grandfather, when he grabbed me underneath my arms and pulled me from the mire and water.

"What kind of warrior are you, Tomas, to scream like a child?" he scolded. "You have stumbled into a beaver's tunnel." There was shouting, laughter, and teasing from all.

"Do not stand still Tomas, as skinny as you and your cousin are, the beaver will think you are young aspen trees and cut you both down with their sharp teeth," Kiko called.

When we made camp I warmed myself by the fire, and that evening we enjoyed the sweet meat of the trout. Others retold the day's events—including my narrow escape from the water spirits—with pleasure and laughter. Pagits enjoyed these stories. I did not.

As darkness came, we built the fires up to keep the chill away. Grandfather came to me. "Do not mind the laughter, Grandson. One day I will tell you of the time your father and your uncle Kiko were boys and were chased up a tree by Old Badger." He smiled, and then I was certain I saw a fear pass over his face as ripples on a pond—perhaps the blackbird, or the fence, I thought. Still, as I went to my robe that night, I wished we could stay always in this place where there was food and beauty.

CHAPTER 4

April 7, 1880
Beaver Creek
Colorado

Topotsuk was selected to lead our first day's hunt. We followed him to a place above the camp, riding into the wind as we climbed so that game above would not know of our coming. We killed several rabbits. Later, we came to the edge of a woods and a large clearing with deep snowdrifts at its far end. Topotsuk raised a hand and signaled silence. He signed the sighting of seven elk. He gestured for us to spread out, and we managed a surround, forcing the animals into the snows where they were bogged down and unable to move well.

I had never killed a large animal, and when I approached a bull caught in the deep drifts, I shook with excitement. As I drew the bowstring back I saw into the animal's eyes. I spoke to him quickly of our needs and gave thanks for his willingness to die should I succeed. I also muttered a small prayer—all these things as I allowed the arrow to fly. It struck the animal in the shoulder and a second point drove deep into his body. He staggered through the snows, then fell upon his side kicking briefly before dying. I left my horse and waded to where he lay. There was cheering and praise from the others who were successful in killing three more of the animals. It was a good day's hunt.

There was a celebration that night for the success of our first hunt and a dance for my killing of the elk. I was made to strip to my waist and the animal's blood was washed over my body. Now I was truly a man, even able to take a wife.

"You must give this meat to another," said Grandfather. "That is the custom. And when you are married, you must be good to your wife."

I thought of the Apache girl in New Mexico.

"You cannot loaf about during the day," Quinch added.

I remembered her brown eyes.

"Or stay in bed in the mornings," said Topotsuk.

Her hands had been warm to my touch.

I received much advice from the others before I cleaned myself and we all went to our robes.

As more game was killed and carried to camp, the women skinned and butchered the animals. They cut the meat into strips and hung it in the sun on racks made from willow branches in the old way so that it would dry. Even the bones of the animals were crushed and boiled, the meat and fat stored in large bags made from skins. The women visited and laughed. They agreed it was a long time since things had been so good. There were venison roasts and ribs over the fire most nights, as we gathered much food to take back to those who remained at the reservation.

Whenever I could, I drew with charcoal from our campfire on the flat faces of rocks, a thing that pleased my mother when she saw the sketches of the hunters carrying an elk. She gave me a small deer hide, and, with a pointed stick and the blood of animals, I drew a picture of the women cutting and drying the meat.

"See the pictures my son makes," she said to the other women, who smiled and nodded in praise.

On the fourth day of the hunt, skies darkened and a cold rain fell. However, we returned with four deer and some rabbits. I went to my robe early.

Pagits leaned into the doorway. "You are an old man hiding under your blankets because of a little rain." I threw a moccasin at him.

After a while, the rain stopped and some of the hunters stood outside, where one of them added dry wood to the fire, stirring it to flames. The glow was reflected on the outside walls of our tent. The men stood or crouched around the fire listening to Topotsuk's flute as they sang and gave thanks for the successful hunt. I imagined my father's strong voice outside, as he would have laughed with the others. When they moved, their shadows danced upon the sides of the tent. From my robe, I reached to catch these fleeting forms on the inside walls. Once, I stared uneasily when I saw the winged shape of a blackbird's shadow. When the shadows slowed, I lay still and listened to Mother breathing softly, and I knew she slept.

Grandfather came into the tent and picked up his robe. "The rain has stopped. It is warmer, and I am going to sleep in the aspen grove beneath the skies where an old man can breathe."

As the fire died, the others went to their lodges. Thunder rumbled softly. I pushed deeper beneath my robe. The stream made a sound like the wind in the trees, and from beneath my covers I smelled the wet pine. Old Coyote cried somewhere in the night. I was grateful for this time.

Later, I awoke and went outside to make water. A warm wind blew softly and I heard the voices of night spirits in the grass and the willows. The moon shone in clearing skies on the high peaks, flooding the campsite. It was bright enough to see the bear on the face of my bracelet. A few sparks rose from the smoldering fire. I hurried back to my robe.

I slept again and dreamed. In my dreams I heard voices—someone singing one of the strange songs I'd heard when Craven held church for some of The People on the reservation. There were other voices swelling into a chorus of sounds—men shouting, horses snorting, their hooves beating upon the ground. Aware it was not a dream, I threw my robe aside. I heard sounds of gunfire and Mother's terrified screams as I fumbled for my bow and the arrows. The thunder of stampeding horses exploded over our camp like a river gone out of its banks. There was the strange smell of kerosene in the air.

"Maricats!" someone screamed.

Our tent was on fire and dragged over. Mother struggled to get outside. I followed, crawling on hands and knees. Then, remembering the paper Craven gave me, I tried to crawl back under the heavy hide. I lost track of Mother and could not find the paper.

Our camp was in turmoil with the attackers riding their horses wildly, our people crying out—pleading. By now, all our lodges were burning. One of the riders drank from a bottle. In the light of the flames I saw Quinch hold his small son up to show the man we were unarmed and meant no harm. The man threw the bottle and rode Quinch and his son down with his horse, firing at them with his gun.

I saw Aunt Kanav and Pagits. Before I could turn to help them, a man on horseback with a large revolver shot both of them. I saw also that our burning tent was dragged away by another rider. Then a man with a beard and long hair like the gray web of spiders rode toward me, reaching down from his saddle to grab my arm, his hand around Father's bracelet. I yelled out and tried to wrench my arm from his grip, then slipped free suddenly when the silver band slid off my wrist.

Released, I ran blindly into the darkness of the aspens and pines.

Striking like a snake, a strong arm reached out from the dark tangle of trees. It wrapped about my shoulders with an iron grip and I was captive again. At the same time a hand was pressed hard on my mouth so that I could not scream. I bit down as the blade of a knife gleamed in the moonlight.

"You have bitten me. Be still." It was Grandfather.

I remained still as I had been taught. The bearded rider was now a short distance from the edge of the aspen grove where we were hidden. I hardly breathed.

The killer's eyes burned white with the fire of the moon. I watched, still as death, as the man grabbed his hat from his head and wiped his forehead with his arm. In the light from a burning tent I saw that his bare skull bore large jagged scars as if he had been cut badly. We watched silently as the rider turned his mount away and, yelling words I did not know, led the others into the night, screaming as they galloped away.

That man has been scalped," Grandfather whispered. "Yet he lives. He has great magic. Bad magic."

When we were certain the attackers would not return, Grandfather made a sound like an owl, and the people began to appear from their hiding places. We found the bodies of my mother, my aunt Kanav, my cousin Pagits, and Quinch. Several others were with wounds. The paper Craven had given me was clutched in Mother's still hand. Her necklace and my father's peace medal had been torn from her neck.

There was great sorrow; loud wailing and keening for the dead. My own grief was enormous. My father's silver bracelet had no power. I had lost those closest to me, the bracelet taken by the man with long hair. I would find it one day. I would find it, and I would find this hairface and remove his entire scalp before destroying him.

It was decided not to bury the bodies in the old way until the incident was reported to the agent and the authorities. It was nearly dawn. Grandfather Cloud Whiskers placed his hand on my shoulder. "Come along, Tomas, we have a long way to ride and much game to carry back to those who remain hungry." In the east, the sun was rising.

When we returned to the reserve, we found the agent Craven had gone away—moved. We were all grateful. We returned to the site with the new agent, two of our headmen, and a number of the soldiers. Because of the condition and position of the bodies of our people, it was seen at once, even by the agent, that the dead were attacked in their tents as they slept. It was the opinion of this man that little concern would be shown by authorities, and it was so. The blue coats and white sheriff told us we must forget the matter and look to our future. I did not tell him that in my future there dwelled a cowardly murderer whose life I would one day take.

The authorities left, and we buried the bodies of the dead in crevices and small caves in the area. I placed my mother's paint bag and sewing tools with her body, along with a handful of sage. I promised her I would avenge her death and continue to be a picture maker to honor her. I put Pagits's bow and arrows by his side. We left quickly then, for their spirits were present and these frightened us. When we returned to our carnivas, my mother's belongings were given away. My grief remained great, as did my hunger for revenge.

CHAPTER 5

May 31, 1880
Southern Ute Reservation
Ignacio, Colorado

I slept.

I dreamed, and in my dreams, the sun rose as granite peaks slashed the skies. The crimson sky ran down dripping from the peaks. A red stream flowed across the land—covering the dry grasses and the yucca and piñon, staining the soft round hills with a sea of red.

"Grandson." I heard Grandfather's voice from far away.

There was the faceless white man with hair spun about his head and his body like the gray webs of spiders. I ran—ran to the far side of the mountain where the red could not follow.

"Wake, Tomas." Holding the flap up, Grandfather crouched in the doorway of our lodge.

I smelled fried bread and burning aspen from the cooking fire but did not want to leave my robe. The summer moons were approaching and already the trees were leafing.

I dreamed often of my mother's death and swore vengeance almost daily on the man who had murdered her. I cursed the whites and the soldiers who had killed my father. Even Azumpitz's medicine failed to drive away my anger and sorrow.

This sadness came at mealtimes when I should have found Mother stirring soup in the large iron pot that hung over the cooking fire. Sadness wrapped itself about my body as a blanket when I remembered Father's strong hands upon my own when he showed me how to string a bow, sharpen a knife, skin a deer. This feeling of great sorrow crept into the tepee at night like Old Coyote so that I lay awake long after Grandfather slept. I wept without tears. I wanted to see the faces of Aunt Kanav and my cousin Pagits—hear their voices, listen to their laughter. I did not think often of Grandfather's pain, though I saw it in the old man's face when, in the morning, he continued to give thanks to his Creator, or in the evening, when he sat by himself and smoked. I was filled only with my rage and my hurt.

One evening as we sat watching the sun go, Cloud Whiskers tried to speak of this sorrow—that joy and sorrow are brothers that travel together. That a man must accept both into his lodge. "I do not want them in mine," I told him angrily.

The following morning, I climbed a hill to a mesa where Pagits and I had built a brush hut in which we became great chiefs and tried to smoke. I carried with me the elk-hide bundle in which father's lance, bow and arrows, and flute were wrapped. As I sat on the ground facing the sun where my father told me the Gods dwelled, I shook my fists at the skies. "What kind of Gods are you," I shouted, "that you have allowed my parents and the others to die like slaughtered sheep?" The sound from my voice was quickly lost in the quiet of the morning.

I removed the red cedar flute from the bundle and blew into it to make a song the way Father had, but the sound that came out was like the squawking of young magpies. I threw the instrument to the ground as my eyes filled with tears—a thing men do not allow. I stood and picked up a dead cedar branch. I ran almost blindly until I came to the large gray trunk of a piñon tree. I beat the tree until the stick broke in my hands, sending pain up my wrist and arm. I fell to my knees sobbing and lay there with eyes closed. Then, I slept.

When the sun stood, the shrill whistle of a hawk overhead in the skies awakened me. I went to where I had thrown the flute and picked it up and wrapped it, hiding the bundle beneath the brush of the hut.

I went often in the morning to this hill and the brush shelter. One day when I blew into the flute, the sounds were like the mourning dove, and I thought I might soon learn to play a song. That day as I huddled behind the walls of the shelter, I was startled to hear a crying sound in the brush behind it. I crawled outside to see a black puppy come to dance, its tail wagging furiously. The dog rolled itself into a ball of fur when I picked it up, then washed my face with its wet tongue. I felt as if a little of my anger had gone away. I placed the animal on the ground again, for my anger was now my strength, and I did not want it to leave.

"Be gone. I do not know you," I scolded the animal. I walked away. The pup followed. "Go away. Do you not see this feather I wear? I am not a child," I shouted.

The pup stared at me, scratched at itself, and tried to bark, falling backward. I laughed. "You are a ferocious thing, aren't you? Then come." I knelt down, scooping up the animal as it ran to me, burying my face against its warm body. I carried it to our lodge. The old man was standing outside hanging wet shirts on a bush to dry.

"What is this you have brought home?" he asked.

"Grandfather. I have found this lost dog up on the mesa."

The old man stroked the pup's forehead. "One of Kiko's bitches has had a litter of pups. It is probably hers."

"It is not Kiko's dog," I said. "I have found him, and he is mine." I placed the pup on the ground, leaned back, and folded my arms.

Grandfather turned away sharply, went to the fire, and removed a pan of fried venison. Returning, he looked at me with his brown eyes, and I wished I had not spoken with such haste. "We shall see about this." He spoke abruptly, then his eyes softened and the anger went from them.

A few days later we went to Uncle Kiko's carniva— Grandfather and I with the puppy. Kiko's other dogs told loudly of our arrival. Kiko waved. "Good day, Cloud Whiskers. Is that a young grizzly bear my nephew is carrying?"

I released the pup, and as we sat upon the grass, Grandfather and Kiko smoked their pipes. The pup went a little distance away to wet the corner of Kiko's tent. Afterward the animal ran to an older female dog that welcomed its return. The two men spoke of the cooling weather, the dropping of the first leaves, and the white governor Pitkin.

"One of our brothers in the north along the Smoking Earth River rode all the way to Denver to see this governor. He spoke to him of lies the white papers spread and the problems The People have with the ranchers. Washington is sending more soldiers to see what is to be done with our cousins in the north."

I thought Grandfather would never speak of the pup.

"My grandson was attacked by this dog while he was on the mesa. I thought it might be one of yours."

Kiko called to the pup, scooped it into his arms, and held it out as he studied it. He turned it around with one hand under its belly, then held its tail out with his other hand. The dog wriggled and tried to lick Kiko's hand. My uncle nodded slowly, as if remembering the skinny tail with fondness. He released the dog and sat back resting his arms across the roll of his belly staring after the pup.

"Yes, it is mine. A favorite. A valuable animal. I'm grateful to you for returning it. I have looked for it."

My heart was heavy.

"It is not much of a dog," Grandfather stared away.

"You are old, Cloud Whiskers—your eyes are weak," Kiko said. "This is a fine animal." He called the pup again, picked it up, and held it close to his chest.

I reached toward the pup and squeezed it softly with my fingers as if measuring its girth, then pinched its skin gently. "The Sioux would not even use this bony animal for their soup. In the short time it has been in our lodge, Uncle, it has done nothing but eat," I said.

Kiko frowned. "This animal will grow into a fine hunter, Tomas—find much game for me," he said.

"In two days all it has found are soup bones and my grandfather's moccasins," I said.

Kiko picked up the dog once more and watched as the small animal licked at his face again. "You see how fond this dog is of me," he said. "It would be a sad thing to lose him."

"You have many dogs, Uncle Kiko," I addressed the man solemnly. "I am going to do you a great favor. Although Grandfather and I have barely enough to live on, we are willing to take this animal off your hands." I held my breath.

"That is a generous thing, Nephew, but this is a favorite of the litter and I cannot give it to you."

I felt as if I'd swallowed a stone.

Kiko laughed loudly and went on speaking, narrowing his eyes. "It will soon be winter and as you see, I do not have enough wood for my fire, for I have been away much this summer since the killings at Beaver Creek. If you will bring me dry piñon so that when the leaves fall I can heat my carniva and my wife can cook, I will let you have this valuable animal."

I scrambled to my feet. "I will bring you the wood you need, Uncle."

"Are you certain, Tomas?" Grandfather asked.

"Even if the snow covers the top of your carniva," I added.

Both men laughed.

I called the pup and it came to me at once. I scooped him up in my arms. "I will call you Badger," I announced. "For you will be ferocious and fearless. Together we will find the men who murdered my mother and the others," I whispered to him. That night, the pup huddled next to me beneath my buffalo robe. When Grandfather came in to go to his own robe, he bent down to look at me. There was a small smile on his face.

CHAPTER 6

June 1, 1880
Southern Ute Reservation
Ignacio, Colorado

I was awakened the following morning by Grandfather yawning loudly, grousing over the noise outside our lodge. "I do not know why our creator made these magpies. Their noise is like the scolding of angry Arapaho women," he said. The dawn light seeped around the edges of the hide door cover on the carniva.

The old man threw back his buffalo robe and rubbed the pain from his arms and knees, pain that came more often now with the winds blowing the yellow leaves from the trees. Badger squirmed beneath my robe. "We must get up now, Tomas, for we are going to ride today to visit my old friend Pazio, who now has a small farm of his own a day's travel from here. He has asked that we come to hunt the deer that are eating his corn. Our new agent has given his permission."

Cloud Whiskers pulled at my robe as he went out from the tent to kindle the fire. I knew he would then walk the short distance to the aspen grove behind the carniva. There, he would pray, reaching skyward to greet the sun and new day with outstretched arms, feeling its brightness on his body, scooping it up, pouring it over his face, washing its warmth over his arms and legs.

I had nothing to say to his Gods. I remained beneath my robe until he returned and I heard him rattling the coffeepot. We ate, then packed provisions and saddled our horses. Side by side, we rode south in the direction of New Mexico. There, where a stream flowed part of the year on his allotment of land, Pazio had managed to create a small farm. This was an accomplishment that Grandfather was certain delighted the government men who talked endlessly of corn and oats and cows.

"What has it come to," Grandfather said, "that a man must work in a field? Once, along the Platte River, we fought together against the Kiowa. On that day a bullet from the gun of a Kiowa warrior struck my old friend Pazio and I rode out to him. There was praise from Sopeta and the others. It was a good fight and we took many horses. Now I am old, and my friend tends a farm, raising corn."

Our trail followed a ways above a creek where cottonwoods greened along its banks. Grandfather began to sing to himself. I held Badger across my saddle in front of me, slowing to ride behind, relaxed and easy, listening to the old man's quivering voice upon the morning.

When the sun was overhead, we angled down a path to the stream, where we found a patch of green grass along its banks. We had seen neither a lizard nor a rattlesnake.

Grandfather paused, turning in his saddle, "We can water the horses and rest."

When we reached the water, the old man slipped from his mount, dropped his blanket, and pulled off his shirt. He kneeled to the stream, and with cupped hands dipped water and drank. He poured it over his head and without warning, turned and threw handfuls of cold water over me. I caught my breath and with a loud war cry threw myself into the water, clothes and all. When I sat up my hair hung in long wet strings down my back. I shook my head like a wet dog then turned to see the old man laughing. I began to laugh with him. Barking, Badger ran back and forth along the creek bank.

In the sunlight, Cloud Whiskers's hair and small mustache were white like wild milkweed seeds, and I was aware suddenly of the bending forward of his shoulders. He saw me staring at the scar hidden in the soft folds of his belly. He touched it.

"An Arapaho lance—before your father was born, even before I made your grandmother my wife." He stared into the blue skies. "She was a beautiful woman, Tomas."

"I wish I could have known her, Grandfather. I want to fight the white soldiers, and these miners who have taken our land," I said. "I would steal their horses away and drive them back to Washington. I want also to find that man who murdered my mother and the others. I will be brave like you have been, Grandfather." I left the stream and stood in the sunlight, dripping water. I picked up a rock and threw it with force against the trunk of a cottonwood tree, and again the tears came into my eyes.

The old man squinted. His voice softened as he spoke. "You were born in the white year 1868 along the banks of the Rio San Juan in the Territory of New Mexico during the month of Falling Leaves. That day, I went to sit and smoke with my friend Azumpitz while I awaited your birth. A great bear came to stand in the skies to the east. Its breath was like fire, its eyes burned as the evening sun." There was the sound of a grandfather's pride in the old man's voice. I went to sit at his side.

"Kwiakati. The bear. It was a sign. A good sign." He leaned

forward to take my arm, gripping it with his fist as he looked into my eyes. "It was a good day for you, Tomas. A good day for The People. Even a good day for Kwiakati. A man, a soldier, is not like the trunk of a tree, Tomas. I believe that in another time you would be a fine warrior, just as your father was."

"Will I never ride in such a fight?" I stripped off my clothing and draped it over a bush.

"I do not think so." His face was sober. "Young men know nothing of wars or soldiers. You are clever and quick. You ride well," he said, now grinning. "For you are like your grandfather. But now you must learn the ways of the whites and go to school and become your mother's picture maker."

He went to his horse and came back with our pack, and we sat in the shade and ate dried venison, hard-boiled eggs, and crackers. "There will be no more wars, Tomas. You and the others must find new ways to be brave, for war is a bad thing for The People."

"No, Grandfather. Why do you say that?"

"There are too many Maricats. Ouray told us in Washington there were lodges of white and black soldiers as thick as the leaves that will soon blossom from the these trees where we are sitting. There are large guns called cannons and many-shots guns such as The People have never seen."

"But you and I can go and find that man who killed my mother."

Grandfather shook his head. "Even the white soldiers have not been able to find that one. How can you and I?"

"They do not look for him, Grandfather. But, I will find him if it takes the rest of my life."

The old man was quiet. He filled his pipe, lit it, and puffed. Smoke rose into the air, and when he spoke again the words came as if from far away. "There is only so much that one man can tell another, Tomas, for wisdom does not come from other men, but from within each person. I believe you think too much about that white man. When I was a young man we rode against our enemies—the Kiowa, the Cheyenne, the Navajo, even the Sioux—to avenge a wrong, the death of a brother or friend. Now that is no longer possible because we live on reservations under the eyes of the white soldiers."

He paused to light his pipe again. "When you sat in the stream and it washed over your body, I saw you laughing and was glad. A man who does not laugh becomes sick inside from his anger. He becomes like dry and barren ground where nothing grows." He scooped up a handful of dirt and let it pour from his hand.

"Like this place we live upon," I said.

Grandfather waved an arm. "There is good here. This green grass that we sit upon. These cottonwood trees and the shade they have given us, where we sit together, you and I—a grandfather and his grandson, whose life was spared by the Gods."

"But how is it possible to laugh when there are many wrongs?"

"Wherever there are men and women it is this way. I have known bad men, even among The People. In the old days, we drove them out of our camp." The old man leaned forward, shook his head at some memory, and the necklace of claws about his neck rattled. "But there is another matter I must speak to you about. The woman who is Red Hair's wife, who lives in the house near the agent, has told me she needs a young man to take care of horses and a few cattle."

"What has this to do with me?"

"This woman knew your mother and has seen you when we go for rations."

"I do not want to take care of livestock for Red Hair."

"That is not the only reason I mention it. The new agent has said you must go with the children and young men to the Indian School at Grand Junction."

"I will not go there. They will cut off my hair and make me wear a soldier's uniform. They do not let one speak in the old ways, but only as the whites."

"This is why we must speak of this."

"I do not want to leave you, Grandfather."

"And I do not want you to go away. That is why I have spoken with this woman. She has two children, a boy and a girl. She has said that if you will come to live with her, she will teach you to read and write the white man's words, for she is a schoolteacher. The agent is her friend, and she will also speak to him so that he will not send you away."

"They are not my friends. They are not friends of The People."

"I believe the Curries are good, Tomas, and mean no harm. You would only stay with them and return home to visit me. If you are to learn about bravery in a white world you must know these things—how to write and speak the words. You do not want to be like your grandfather and the others, growing corn in ground where only cactus and soap weed should live."

I listened and remembered a time I went with my father and the other men to catch wild horses. We drove the animals into a small canyon where there was no way out. "If you say it, I will go and see this woman. But I want to come to visit you, Grandfather."

"I would like that, Tomas."

We killed no deer at Pazio's farm, and in two sleeps we returned home.

CHAPTER 7

June 4, 1880
Southern Ute Agency
Ignacio, Colorado

Badger sat watching as I washed with the soap from Washington. Grandfather hovered about me like a red-tailed hawk.

"Are you certain this soap is not for our horses, Grandfather, or for tanning the deer hide?" I held my nose.

"You must wash well, Tomas, for you remember what old Craven said before he went away, that Maricats do not like dirty boys." The old man grinned and went to fetch more water from the campfire. I squirmed and sputtered when he poured it over my head and body. When he thought I was clean, he allowed me to dress. I brushed my hair with the brush Mother used on Father's hair, and in my mind and heart I saw him take Mother's hand.

"That agent should not have let us leave the reservation. We should have gone hungry," I muttered.

"What do you say, Grandson?"

"I said nothing, Grandfather." *I will have revenge,* I told myself.

Grandfather Cloud Whiskers gave me one of his own overshirts. I rolled the shirtsleeves up, then put on new elk-hide moccasins with bright colored beads Mother decorated for me. Grandfather was staring at me, his eyes, however, seeing beyond me—perhaps to another time and place.

Red Hair's woman was hanging clothes alongside the house on a rope tied between trees. Two children chased a large, shaggy dog. Badger began to whine and bark. I held him tightly.

"You may get down, Tomas," Grandfather spoke.

I slid from my horse, tying the animal's reins to a post. The woman saw us, smiled, and dropped an armful of clothing into a basket. The children stared at Grandfather and me. I looked at the ground. The large dog ran around barking as Badger squirmed in my arms.

"Be still, McKeever," the woman spoke to the dog as it came toward us, wagging its tail. Grandfather squatted to take the dog's head in his arms and stroke its fur. The children, a girl my age and her younger brother, whispered to one another. Was I clean enough? Why were they staring at me?

"A fine animal, but a strange name," Grandfather said.

"A friend of Major Currie gave the dog to us when we came west. He was a Scotsman so we named the animal McKeever. The Major has gone to Denver to meet my brother, Frank McCants. Frank will serve as an interpreter when General Hatch arrives in a few weeks to speak with your people of the trouble in the north."

I glanced up quickly. The woman was smiling at me. Had I braided my hair improperly?

"You may put your dog down, Tomas," Grandfather said. He turned to the woman. "I know your brother. He has always been our friend—a friend of The People."

When I placed Badger on the ground, the larger animal moved to tower nose to nose with him. Then they jumped back from one another and began to chase each other. The children laughed. Even I grinned as the dogs ran wildly about—Badger stumbling on his stubby legs, rolling over the ground.

The white woman spoke to Cloud Whiskers in Spanish. She put her hand out to take his hand. I waited anxiously, for I knew the old man did not approve of this touching.

"Cloud Whiskers." She shook Grandfather's hand. Her hair was the color of grass that has turned light brown during the first moon of fall. Her eyes were as the morning sky. She turned to the children. "Robert. You and Suzan please show Tomas the animals."

There were three horses within a small corral. Two cows were penned next to the horses. A few chickens pecked about the yard. Mrs. Currie and Grandfather followed.

"This is where you'll stay, Tomas." Suzan gestured toward a small cabin. It was a single room. Within were a bed, a nightstand, and a small table with a pitcher and bowl.

Grandfather spoke to the woman. "My grandson has never seen the white man's bed."

The woman spoke to the boy. Robert grinned, then he lay down upon the bed as one lies upon the ground. He rolled about, and closed his eyes as if sleeping. He began to snore loudly. "My grandfather snores." I said without thinking. Mrs. Currie laughed. Even Grandfather laughed. I laughed. The children laughed, too, although they did not understand my words. It was good.

"This," grandfather Cloud Whiskers said to me, "is how the whites sleep—upon a bed." "You will have to learn to sleep upon this bed, Grandson."

I would sleep upon the floor in my buffalo robe, but I would not snore like the old man.

The woman gave Cloud Whiskers coffee with sugar and some sweet breads. She gave us milk, although I wanted coffee. I ate three of the breads.

"My grandson eats like a small bear." Grandfather patted my stomach. Then he stood and said he must leave. He put his hand on my shoulder. "I will come back for you in this many sleeps." He held up all his fingers.

That night it was a difficult thing to sleep in the small house. Again I did not feel brave. What would happen to The People when the white general came? Would the soldiers come with their cannons and many-shots guns? And swords?

Apart from chores, I spent most of my time with Robert and Suzan, while Red Hair's wife, Mary, held school for us in their home. I learned quickly to count numbers and speak many of the Maricats' words. Robert and Suzan helped me to remember the numbers and to say these words.

There were books with pictures the colors of the rainbow. I wanted to know all of the Maricats' words. I believed their magic would help me one day to find the murderous Gray Hair. Mrs. Currie showed me how to make my name and other words on paper with a pencil. She gave me paper from some of the rations at the agency. As I moved the pencil on the paper, I made marks, like the marks of embers on the rocks, as I had that day of the hunt.

A few days later, it began to rain hard. We sat at a pine table in the kitchen. A fire burned in the cookstove. Mrs. Currie dumped a box of colored sticks on the table. I chose one. "They are crayons." Suzan repeated the word: "Cray-ons."

"Cray-ons," I replied. I tasted one and quickly spit it out. She and Robert laughed. "Candy?" I asked.

"No, Tomas. They are not to eat," she said. She picked one up and scratched with it on paper. It was the color of a sunset. I did the same. It was the color of blood. Suzan showed me how to use the crayons.

Mrs. Currie went into the front room where she played her piano. I had never heard music like this, not even from my father's flute. It was as if Azumpitz had cast a spell on me, for when I closed my eyes, I saw green valleys, a stream, and mountain peaks as in a dream.

I was not aware of my friends at the table. I moved the crayons upon the paper. Soon I was climbing again with Cousin Pagits in the sunlight among the rocks above the camp where my mother and my aunt were cutting venison. I saw the colored beads on Mother's dress, the green turquoise in Aunt Kanav's silver earrings, the sky above the Shining Mountains after a summer rain, the colors my people made from the earth and fruits to paint themselves. There were the grays and greens of pines, piñon trees, sage, and yucca. There were blood-red sunrises, lavender skies at evening, oranges and yellows of earth, blues of the midday sky. I was not aware that the music had stopped, that Mrs. Currie stood over me. The room was nearly dark, the rain still falling.

"Tomas."

I saw only the bright colors as they went from my hands to the paper.

"Tomas."

I looked up to see this woman standing over me. Suzan was watching from across the table. Robert was asleep in a large chair. "This is very well done," Mrs. Curry said. "I am amazed."

I thought I had done something to make her angry. She spoke again and placed her hand on my shoulder. "Good, Tomas. Good work." She patted my back.

"You are an artist, Tomas," Suzan said. "He will be our artist, won't he, Mother?"

I stared down at the brown paper and saw the things that came from the crayons, and was frightened. Was I a picture maker? There were the white hills above Beaver Creek, Pagits playing on the rocks, the killing of elk and deer, Mother and the other women drying venison on a rack. There was a fire burning, a moon, the murderers on horseback, and a white man without a face—his long, stringy hair and beard that dragged across the ground.

I saw the bodies of my mother, my aunt, and my cousin. The drawings were crude but recognizable to Mary Currie who, I learned, knew of the killings. I stood, staring down at them, and the blackness that was lodged in my gut like a great heaviness began to swell within my chest, wrapping itself about my heart, before it spilled out of me. My body shook, and I turned away from this thing upon the paper, falling against the body of the woman who now held me with her arms as one of her own. I cried, the darkness passed, and I was as tired as if I had walked many miles. Mary Currie led me to a divan and sat by me until I slept.

CHAPTER 8

August 17, 1880
Southern Ute Reservation
Ignacio, Colorado

Many moons had passed since the killing of the agent Meeker and the taking of the agency women. Anger and fear among the settlers and prospectors had been made greater by lies told by the governor, the newspapers, and others. Meetings with The People, the white general Hatch, and the men from Washington were to be held at Los Pinos during the month of Cricket Sings. Red Hair said there would be many soldiers there.

When I returned to Grandfather's lodge after time with the Curries, the old man was stirring a pot of stew over the campfire. I showed him my drawings. "These are fine drawings, Grandson. I believe you have been given a gift." I was pleased with Grandfather's words.

"Our friend Frank McCants has brought a picture maker from Denver with him," Grandfather said. "You must show him these. I believe you will like McCants, Tomas. He has good hands and I think his heart is worthy. He will speak well for us. I don't know about the other one. His hands are soft like goat teats."

I looked at my own hands.

"I knew a man like that once," Azumpitz said. "A paka-wici with hands like a young woman's. He made clay pots and wove blankets." The shaman shook his head, laughing softly. "He was a brave man, though."

Grandfather dipped stew from the iron pot. I thought his face was thinner, more wrinkled. When he breathed it seemed difficult for him, and I saw some small pain in his face. I tasted the stew and said, "This meat is strange. It is not venison or elk."

"Chatta's old woman gave me this meat," Grandfather said. "It is from one of the white rancher's cows that strayed onto our land. Chatta does not see well and thought it was a buffalo."

Azumpitz laughed. "Chew it well, Tomas, for it is like horse hide."

"Will The People be moved away?" I asked.

"There is talk," the old man said. "The chiefs and The People say they will not leave."

"Uncle Kiko would rather die than move from the land," I said.

"Kiko is a good man, Tomas, but I don't think he wants to die yet. He is too fond of biscuits and horse racing."

Grandfather tipped the bowl to his lips and sipped the last drops of liquid, wiping his mouth and thin mustache with his sleeve.

Azumpitz belched loudly and turned to me. "It is from the cow," he explained.

Grandfather stared up at the sky. A large hawk rode the air currents above a ridge. The old man placed a hand on my shoulder. "Grandson. You and I have spoken of how a young man may go off by himself and seek his power from the Gods. If he has a good dream he will return with this power."

"My father sent me into the woods when I was a boy," Azumpitz said. "The first night there was a great storm with rain and lightning. The trees bent to the ground. It was a fearful thing. While I fasted, a little green man came out from his house in the earth and we visited until dawn. We sang together and he gave me songs and the powers to heal others. That is how I became a shaman." Azumpitz tapped his pipe gently into the palm of his hand and turned to Grandfather.

"My first night alone was not good," Grandfather said. "The darkness was so great I could not see even the flames from the small warming fire in front of me. There were bad noises as the animals of the forest gathered in the darkness. I trembled much and thought the night would never end. During the second night, it was worse. On the third day, I rode upon the wings of a great hawk, seeing all of the land and The Shining Mountains. I received my power during this flight. I have tried to use this power wisely."

Stories told by these two old men did not frighten me. I was not afraid of darkness, or great noises. Not even flying as a bird.

"Sakwamatutaci."

Grandfather spoke my Ute name slow, softly. I had not heard this name often since the death of my mother. She told me once that when she carried me in her belly, a beautiful hummingbird came to sit on a tree branch and spoke to her. She made a song of this tiny bird's words and sang the words to me when I hung in my cradleboard—swayed to sleep by the breezes. I heard Grandfather's voice again. "My father sent me, and I sent your father, when he was young. I will send you, Grandson."

"I have been thinking of this thing, Grandfather, and I would like to go," I said, although I did not believe in his Gods.

"Where will you go?" Azumpitz asked.

"There is a place two sleeps from here beyond the mesa in that direction." I pointed into the sky and at the hawk still circling there. "A small stream flows at the base of red cliffs. There is a shallow cave above where the Ancient Ones lived. The piñon trees are twisted and wrinkled as old people. When I was a small boy, I went there once during the Fruit Moon when my mother and the other women gathered piñon nuts and gooseberries. I have wanted to return."

"I have been there," Azumpits said. "A place of many snakes. You must watch out for old Tukwuapi, for his fangs bring pain and even death."

"I will ask Hawk to guide you and watch over you, my boy," Grandfather said.

Three sleeps passed, and I rose on a morning before the sun was up so that I might travel far before the heat of day became great. Grandfather packed a parfleche with dried fruit and venison and filled an old army canteen for me. Once at my destination, I would fast. I held Badger as I said good-bye to him. Grandfather embraced me, watching as I mounted Pinto and rode away.

By midmorning the sun's heat had driven the animals to shade and burrow. Even the birds had gone away. Only Hawk, who I now called friend, remained in the skies, flying in ever-widening circles until she could no longer be seen, then reappearing suddenly. I removed my shirt and blanket, tying both behind the saddle. Although I did not like this heat, I knew it would drive the rattlesnakes underground.

The sun climbed and the heat became so great that sweat ran into my eyes. I stopped to rest and drink beneath the shade of an ancient juniper tree. Leaning back against its large trunk, I smelled suddenly the odor of green weeds that grow along the riverbank. There was no river here and nothing green on this ground but yucca and cactus. I removed the lid from the canteen and drank, studying the writhing trunk of the aged tree from its top branches downward to where its large gray roots arched up from the ground. Pinto snorted.

The serpentine tree trunk had pushed its way up out of the dry earth long ago, shoving fragments of stone into a pile around its trunk. Through blurred eyes, I saw one scaled, knurled old root, the size of my arm, stretch from the main trunk to lie across the baked ground. I wiped my eyes dry with my arm. The root moved. I did not breathe, then slowly lowered my arm as I heard the rattle of death. Tukwuapi—the rattlesnake.

The hair on the back of my neck rose, and my blood left my body as the snake separated itself from the tree's roots to slip slowly over stones and clay toward my outstretched bare leg. I remained still as the thing slid close to my foot, tongue flicking, along the right side of my body. The muscles in my neck and back knotted. I tried to breathe without movement, my heart pounding violently as words poured from my heart to the Gods I did not believe in. "Give me wings of the hawk to fly if you are there," I whispered. Instead the snake slid slowly along my bare thigh.

I had seen the wounds Tukwuapi inflicted on a woman in our camp once while she gathered berries. The pain from its fangs was great. The tree and I were now one. The snake grinned. "Who is it that you whisper your prayers to?" it hissed.

My body turned to water. I did not move but stared at it. "What do you say, Tukwuapi?" my voice croaked dryly.

"Why do you ask for wings, Sakwamatutaci? Would you be a bird or a man? And who is there to hear your pleading?" Snake's soft laughter was like the rustling of dry weeds. "Do you seek help from the fantasies of foolish old men?"

"They are not foolish old men, Tukwuapi, but elders— good and wise," I said, my own voice strangled, as if by dry dust. "Their words have been a comfort when I have sought guidance."

"You do not need their archaic guidance, Tomas. Nor do you need their outworn Gods, for you are already wise beyond your age. Would that I had this wisdom you possess."

I moved my hand slowly as the snail seeking water, until I grasped where my father's bracelet once was. A warmth moved up my arm and through my body, and I saw his face and felt his presence.

"I can be your friend, Tomas. I will give you guidance that is real."

"With all due respect, Tukwuapi, I do not wish for your aid, but that you go away."

The snake hissed, coiled, and shook his rattles. At their sound, Hawk dove from her perch, screaming at the snake. Tukwuapi spit at me, then turned away, slithering without haste toward the rocks. Hawk was back on her perch, flapping her wings.

Weak and trembling, I made myself stand, and when I had recovered my strength, I mounted the pony. Hawk flew, going before me. I gripped my wrist where Father's bracelet once was and stared skyward at the bird's easy flight.

"Thank you." I breathed the words to a fiery sun.

I rode far the rest of that day, and in the evening I descended from the mesa into a small valley where the stream flowed. The water was cold and clear and I washed my face and body. I found a place where the sand was piled, spread my blanket over it and sat to eat the last of my dried venison and bread. The few pines and piñon trees outlined along the ridge pierced the red and lavender skies like stone points. Slowly, the remaining light faded into black night as Old Coyote called. Darkness came. I lay down, covered myself, and slept.

CHAPTER 9

August 19–20, 1880
Southern Ute Reservation
Ignacio, Colorado

The night passed, and I woke to see Hawk perched on the top branch of a large cottonwood tree alongside the stream. When I had washed, we traveled south along the base of the red cliffs. Scrub oak and piñon grew here, and I kept an eye out for Snake. At times our way wandered from the water, then returned. We rode all day, stopping only that I might let Pinto drink and graze.

The sun was low when I reached my destination. I crossed the stream to the opposite bank, hobbled Pinto, and climbed a trail worn by the feet of the Long Ago People. A sadness came to me again, for this was where we had picked berries and piñon nuts. Even now the bushes along the banks of the stream were covered with green currants and wild gooseberries. The way led to a ledge overlooking the stream and the valley. In a pool below, I could see the shadows of fish. A cool breeze touched my face. It was a sacred place with many good forces. Chips of chert and flint lay on the ledge where they were dropped from the hands of ancient arrow makers from many winters past. I found a whole point and two broken pots.

The sun dropped behind the ridge, and I went beneath a

smoke-stained stone overhang and sat leaning back against a rock wall.

The relics were good signs, and I thanked Hawk again for protecting me from Snake. There was no food left. I covered my legs and body with my blanket and closed my eyes, hearing the stream and the breezes and the birds. Then the bird sounds were hushed and I heard only the stream. I watched the last of Sun's color go from the skies, seeing Hawk on the branch of a piñon tree. Bird and tree were silhouetted against the little light remaining.

The following night, my mind wandered between consciousness and sleep, and once, I smelled Mother's cooking on the night air—her buffalo roasts, rich brown gravies, wild onions, carrots, and potatoes. I tasted Mrs. Currie's hot biscuits sopped in meat gravy. Even in this dry air, my mouth watered at the thought of the teacher's sweet cakes made with sugar and chocolate.

There were other hungers in one's life.

I saw clearly my father, mother, aunt Kanav, and Pagits in the deepening shadows. I reached out, calling their names, but they went away.

"I am hungry," I whispered to Hawk, as I closed my eyes.

"I have been hungry," Hawk replied softly, the sound of her voice a remembered dream from a faraway time. "One hot, dry summer," she continued, "with little rain, only dry grasshoppers to eat, I flew far, many sleeps, to the land of the Yutas so that I would not starve. I recall one day—"

I heard no more from my friend, for I slept.

During the dark night before the dawn of the third day, I was awakened by Wind's long, chilling fingers ripping at the thin blanket wrapped about my body. As it blew against the trees and howled along the canyon walls, it was like the sounds of many coyotes. In the rubbing of tree branches I heard the singing of the Long Ago People.

I crouched close to the wall, clutching my blanket to my body with one hand, holding part of it over my head and face to hide from Wind's fury. Then Wind was gone away and after a moment, I dropped the blanket from my face.

A stillness settled over everything. Moonlight flooded the land with white light, washing trees and rocks. I could not hear the noise of water against the rocks in the stream below or the night birds in the trees or even the spirits in the grass. The only sound was the beat of my heart and the whisper of my breath as it entered and left my body.

A large, dark form rose to stand against the first light, and I smelled a rank odor—a sour smell of caves where large animals live. It grew stronger as the form moved closer until its stench enveloped me. I wanted to run, but my legs were the buffalo grass of prairies. I drew my head down and hunched my shoulders. I was like the turtle. I crossed my arms against my chest so that my heart would not fly out from my fear. I am a man, I told myself. I am not afraid.

I pulled my knees up against my stomach where a knot had grown as a large fist. I was not brave and wanted to be away from this place, safe with Grandfather. I was called back from my thoughts as I heard the moccasin feet scraping softly across the stone floor. The figure stood only a few feet from me. Once more I heard the mocking laughter of the Long Ago People from the rocks and from the many dark crevices. If there are Gods, let them save me from death, I prayed.

The thing stood over me, its shaggy head touching the roof of the ledge that was my shelter. As it bent down, I saw the glowing eyes of a giant grizzly bear peering at me. Wild guttural sounds came from its long snout. I had no weapon, not a stone or a stick to defend myself. With my arms I felt behind myself, praying that the rock wall would open and swallow me. I was to be killed and would never see Grandfather again. In my terror I recalled the man who killed my mother and the others—saw again the ax raised, the slayer's face hidden in its tangle of webs. Saw the bodies of my family.

The bear spoke. "I have been waiting for you, Tomas Dequine." How could this animal know my name? How could it speak? "My child has fallen into a deep hole," the bear continued, "made by the ones seeking gold. The little one calls for me, but I am unable to free him and I fear he will soon die."

"What can I do?" I gasped. Only a little of my fear was gone.

"Hawk has talked of your pain, Tomas. She has also told me that you are a clever young man."

"Hawk is too generous with her praise," I replied. "What else has this bird told you?"

"That you seek revenge against the Gray Hair for the killing of your mother and the others. If you free my child, we will speak of these things."

"I do not know what I can do, but if you will lead me to this place, I will see."

"Climb upon my back," the bear said.

My fear was great again as I climbed onto the animal, clinging to its long fur while it carried me through the night to a place in the forest where the trees had been cleared away and the ground torn up by prospectors. In the moonlight, I saw the dark outlines of a large pit and heard the soft whimpering of the bear-child from below.

Peering into the opening, I saw the form of the cub. As I leaned over, one of many stones piled around its edge was dislodged. It rolled into the hole. The cub moved quickly out of the way as the stone crashed into the bottom of the crater. After a moment the cub climbed up on the stone and, leaning against the side of the pit, began to cry again.

"Hawk was right. You are clever, Tomas," Bear said, as she nudged a second stone into the hole. Again, the cub stood aside. I lifted another stone and dropped it carefully. One by one, Bear and I replaced many stones. Working through the night, we filled the hole to a point where the cub was able to climb to safety. Mother Bear nuzzled the body of her offspring, then, content that the child was unharmed, turned to me.

"Tomas Dequine, the Great Creator who made all things has led you to the beginning of a wisdom that lies as a seed within each man and woman. In this wisdom these rocks became stepping stones, and out of a dark pit you have brought my child that it might grow old and enjoy the fruits of life upon this earth. Tomas, you will now be called The Boy Who Slept with Bears."

As the cub moved from its mother, it turned and looked back, then ambled into the night. The grizzly looked at me again.

"The Boy Who Slept with Bears, your way will be narrow and steep. However, your quest for revenge for that one who killed your parents and the others will be satisfied. It will be accomplished through the bow, the arrows, and the lance that belonged to your father. Do not lose them."

Later, when I opened my eyes, a gentle rain was falling over the ledge and on the land. Gradually the skies cleared, and the sun shone on the remaining drops of rain like small gold coins. The perfume from grass and wildflowers and trees was heavy over the land. I had to return home.

CHAPTER 10

August 25, 1880
Southern Ute Reservation
Ignacio, Colorado

During "part summer, part fall—the time of cricket sings," many of The People were gathered to hear again more words of Washington.

"What has happened to The People, Tomas?" Grandfather asked. "Where have so many winters gone?"

He grunted with discomfort from the pain in his hips and thighs when he hunkered down upon the ground. He stared into the council fire as if seeing beyond the flames to another time and place. There was a sadness in the voice of the old warrior. It had been decided by Washington that our Ute cousins in the north were to be moved from their ancient home where the spirits of their relatives dwelled to a distant place in Utah. This, because of the murder of Meeker and his farmhands, and the taking of the white women now returned. There was great sorrow among all The People for this. Nicigat, called Jack, was already in Fort Leavenworth Prison. No one cared that my father was killed, nor had the soldiers or Washington found the men who killed my mother and the others.

Ouray, who Washington said was chief of all the Utes, was

ill. He and his band arrived and camped north of the agency buildings. Grandfather pointed out other old friends present. "There is Tapoche, one of our Capote chiefs," Grandfather spoke quietly. "That man over there, Grandson, with the feathers of the eagle tied to his braids, is Ignacio of the Weeminuche, and there is Aiguillar of the Muache. There sitting with the Maricats is my old companion Buckskin Charlie. It's said that Ouray is dying and has asked Charlie to take over as chief of all The People. That beautiful woman with them is Ouray's wife, Chipita, who is always at the side of her husband.

Ouray's swollen belly showed beneath the beaded buckskin clothing he had returned to wearing. His face was haggard— worn from pain. The white doctors and his medicine man had not been able to make his sickness go away.

"The tall man with the commissioners is my old friend McCants," Grandfather said. "He is Mrs. Currie's brother. He is a rancher who will make the words of Washington into our language. He speaks straight and I have great respect for him," the old man continued. "He was a soldier and fought in the white man's war. He has long been a friend of the Ute."

Later that night, when the stars came out, the words of the commission were being discussed angrily around the many small fires that lighted the area where the bands were camped. Grandfather and I sat away from the others at our own fire. I was fearful of the words spoken during the day by the men from Washington. "Must all of The People move away?" I asked him.

"They have decided the southern bands may remain here," Grandfather replied. "But they want to divide what is left of this bit of ground they have given us into small farms so that each man might become a farmer." Grandfather stirred onions as he cooked one of the pieces of beef the new agent had given to all of the participants. "Tell me, Grandson, how has it gone—this learning the white language from the Currie woman?"

"I am able to speak some English. You yourself have taught me some Spanish, and I can write some of the white words," I said. *These things would help me to find the hairface,* I thought.

"You are still making pictures?"

"Yes," I replied. "I have learned much while staying with the Curries. I know how to draw with pencils and crayons," I said. I had even made a drawing of the hairface, though I did not say so.

"When you learn the white words and make the pictures, do you remember the ways of your fathers and grandfathers?" the old man asked.

"Yes," I told him. "I will remember them always." As I will remember the night my mother was murdered.

"You frown, Grandson."

"It is the smoke, Grandfather," I lied. I moved farther from the flames.

"That man Comstock who has come with McCants says that you have a gift to make pictures as he does. I don't know what good this is, but he tells me it has some value. He says that you ought to go to a school in Denver where these things are taught."

"I do not want to go to a school, Grandfather."

"I did not say you had to go to a school, but you must not close your mind to this. I am old, Tomas. My eyes have become cloudy, and one day I will go to the place where the rest of the old ones have gone, and you will be alone." He grinned suddenly. "Unless you find a good-looking woman." He rubbed my head. "Like your grandmother," he added.

"You are not going away, Grandfather, and I do not want to talk about these things," I said. As we ate and the old man continued to speak, my mind traveled back to New Mexico and the girl. We stood by the side of a beaver dam one evening as the sun was going down. Though I was not yet a man, she kissed me lightly on my cheek. A fragrance flowed from her long hair, one I could not forget.

Grandfather coughed. "We must speak of them, Grandson. Our way is changing and we cannot stop this, any more than we can prevent the leaves from falling. The days of our people living free as they used to are gone. I don't know what will become of us. Even if we refused to sign this new paper from Washington, it will not stop change."

"How did you know that you wanted Grandmother for your wife?" I asked the old man.

"What?" He looked up, startled.

"Grandmother," I repeated. "How did you know she would be your wife?"

"You have not been listening to me, Tomas," he scolded. "We were speaking of change."

"We might fight the soldiers," I said, returning to the subject.

"We have spoken of this, Tomas. We would be destroyed." Grandfather looked into my eyes, smiling. He leaned forward, brushing my cheek with his finger. His voice was soft. "A man knows he is in love with a woman when his heart agrees with his eyes, when he cannot eat or sleep."

Grandfather was right. About fighting and about one's heart. My heart spent much time with this girl.

A figure came from the darkness into the circle of our firelight. It was the interpreter, McCants. "Good evening, Cloud Whiskers."

"McCants." Grandfather stood slowly and motioned the man to sit. "Have you eaten?"

"Yes, my friend. I just want to talk with you," McCants said.

"This is my grandson, McCants. His head is filled with thoughts of pretty Apache girls this evening," Grandfather laughed.

"Only one Apache girl," I said.

"I know of this young man." McCants took my hand. "My sister, Mrs. Currie, speaks well of your learning, Tomas, and your ability to draw." McCants continued, speaking to Grandfather. "You know that Ouray is very ill, Cloud Whiskers. The white doctors say he may die even before the talks are over. The chief has sent the doctors away and brought in his own medicine man again."

"I am sorry to hear this," Grandfather said.

"When he dies, Cloud Whiskers, many are afraid the Utes will not sign the agreement. I have been asked by Commissioner Manypenny to speak to some of the headmen to convince them that it is best for them to sign this new treaty. I don't see any other way, my friend."

"I don't like this, McCants, but I know that we have little choice," Grandfather said.

I stood and walked a little distance away to hide my anger at the words of McCants and Grandfather.

"The White River and Uncompahgre Utes will be moved to Utah by Colonel Mackenzie. He has nine companies of infantry. Many, many men," McCants said. Grandfather remained silent. "As you know, your Capote brothers, the Weeminuches and Muaches, will be allowed to stay here in the south on the reservation. I wanted you to know what is going on."

Grandfather called to me. "Tomas, go and find your uncle Kiko. He was going to visit with Aiguillar at the west side of the camp. Ask him if he will come to my lodge." As I passed out of the firelight, I turned to look back and saw the old man lighting his pipe, and I was sure there were more words he would have with the white rancher. Words I should not share.

That evening after McCants left and we went to our robes, Grandfather spoke to me in the darkness of our lodge. "Tomas, there is a thing that weighs upon my mind and heart."

"Yes, Grandfather." There was a trembling in the old man's voice that I had noticed earlier.

"I have not been well. There is blood that comes at times when I cough. The doctor from Fort Lewis says that I have a disease of the lungs. I do not remember what he called it." I would not listen to the old man. If I refused to answer him, his words would go away. An ember from our warming fire sparked.

"Are you asleep, Grandson?"

"No, I am not sleeping, Grandfather," I said softly.

"I have spoken with McCants, asking him if you might go to his ranch and live with him and his woman until this trouble is over. It is in the place called South Park. We used to stop there on our way to hunt the blackhorns east of Denver. You would be safe there and could learn more the ways of the Maricats."

I would not speak. I closed my eyes, pretending sleep. I knew well the white ways. These ways had taken my mother and father from my life. I had promised my mother to avenge her death by finding the Long Hair with the snow eyes.

"Do you hear me, Tomas?"

Somewhere in the night an owl hooted. There was the sound of thunder and wind, a smell of distant rain, even above our smoldering fire. One cannot know the paths the Gods will lead him down during his lifetime. I was about to travel new trails in a strange and unfamiliar world. I slept with my eyes open, wondering at the promises of Kwiakati. Badger nuzzled against my side, and I wrapped my arms around him.

CHAPTER 11

September 3, 1880
Howbert
South Park, Colorado

When the talking with Washington had ended, I packed my parfleche with my few belongings. I carried also the elk-skin bundle containing my father's bow, arrows, lance, and flute. I would need these weapons for my revenge when I found the bearded white man with the scalping scar.

After speaking with her brother, Frank McCants, Mrs. Currie agreed not to cut my hair. They bought me new clothing at Animas City. The man on the train even let me take Badger with me. I said good-bye to the old man, and with Frank, Comstock, and Badger, left for Alamosa by stagecoach where we would board the train to South Park and Frank McCantses' ranch near Black Mountain.

I was angry with Grandfather for sending me to live in the square house of the whites. My fear of these things was greater than any I had known, though I kept this to myself. I thought I would rather face a war party of Kiowa and Arapaho than leave Grandfather and the others to come live with the white rancher and his wife. Many times during the trip I wanted to jump from the train with Badger and return home.

The train bucked, swayed, and screamed like the wild horses

my people went to catch when I was young. A white stallion threw me from his back many times that day. My arms and legs ached, my back was sore, and I walked for days as an old man. It was the same riding on this train.

We passed through a wide valley, by the side of a river the whites call the Arkansas. There were great snowcapped peaks to the west.

Alex Comstock came to sit by me. "Those mountains divide the waters from the rain and melting snows that fall upon all the land," he told me. "The waters then flow to the east and west." He pointed to the two directions. "The waters on this side flow down creeks, into rivers, and then flow all the way to the east, even beyond the place called Washington, to a great ocean where the sun comes up. In the other direction they flow to the ocean where the sun goes down."

"This place was a favorite hunting ground for some of my people," I told Comstock.

He opened a satchel to remove a package wrapped in brown paper tied with a string. "A small gift for you, Tomas." I tore the paper from the package and was pleased to find a new box of crayons and a ledger book to make pictures in. "I have seen your drawings. You draw well, and I believe with practice you could become a fine artist," he said. "There are many Indian artists."

"I would like that," I told him.

"I will be happy to help you." Comstock lit his pipe as he spoke. "In the white year 1875 when you were a small boy, there was much trouble between the settlers and the Cheyenne and Kiowa. There were others, but I do not recall their names."

"I know of this trouble," I said.

"Washington took chiefs and a number of braves in chains on the iron rails to a prison far away in the direction of the sun.

To a place called Florida," Comstock said. "With the chains removed, these men learned to draw and paint while there, and they sold many of their drawings and paintings. They made friends there, too. Sadly, some of them died without seeing their home and families again." I felt bad for those people, but I was glad they had learned to draw.

Frank told me I was not to escape learning to read and write the words of the Maricats' language. He told me Red Hair's woman, Mary Currie, gave the study books to Frank's wife, Elizabeth, who had also been a schoolteacher, and I knew my schooling was to continue at the ranch. There was no way out of this for me. Not yet.

There were many stops along the way for miners and other travelers. Frank and Comstock got off at one of these while waiting for the train to be filled with water. I allowed Badger to go and relieve himself, and then returned to the train, for a cold rain was falling from dark skies.

It was then I saw him—long gray strings of hair dripping from beneath his hat. His beard was soaked. He climbed onto the train carrying a rifle and large bag. He had not seen me yet. My heart leapt, beating as the hooves of a wild stallion. He was the Gray Hair—the angry man I'd seen pounding Craven's desk on the day the agent gave me the paper so we could go and hunt. I held my breath. Gray Hair removed his hat, slapped it against his pants leg, and sat down. I tried to see the top of his head where the jagged scar might be. Then he looked up and his cold gray eyes stared into mine. I turned away to peer out the window at my side. When I turned around, his rain-soaked hat was back on his head.

I did not see the boy at my side until he spoke to me. He was older and taller than I was. "What you looking at, Indian? And what's a Indian doing on a railroad train in South Park with a damn dog? This ain't no cattle car." The boy grinned. "Hell, you

don't speak English, so you don't even know what I'm saying."
His eyes were gray also. His voice was unfriendly. Badger gave
a low growl. I looked down at my hands and said nothing, and
the boy went to sit by the Long Hair.

I clenched my fists in anger. I closed my eyes. I heard in
my head the screams and saw again my people dying in the
bright moonlight of that night. Was the Long Hair their killer?
Yes. He was. He had to be, I thought. If I had a large knife, I
would—. "What's wrong with you, Tomas?" Frank surprised
me as he and Comstock sat down again. The train jerked to a
start.

"Nothing is wrong," I lied.

CHAPTER 12

September 5, 1880
McCants Ranch
South Park, Colorado

"Trout Creek Pass!" The conductor bellowed. The train screeched to a stop. Two men got off. The rain had ended. Frank and Alex went outside again to walk. I followed them.

Frank pointed below. "That's South Park, Tomas, but you can't see much today for all the fog." A thick mist filled the park so that only the tops of hills and peaks showed like islands—a sight I would remember.

I came here as a boy with my father and grandfather, but I was too young then to remember it well. Grandfather told me that the Makita from the place called Dakota and the Kwumaci and others from the plains came here to hunt and gather the iapi—what the whites call "salt." Our people fought with them and chased them from the park. If they came after us, we fled back into the mountains where they could not catch us, for we were more skilled in riding the steep terrain.

"Board!" The conductor waved us back to the train. We had begun the slow trip downhill when I saw through the train window the shape of a mountaintop standing above the others. It was a dark lodge—where I was certain many spirits dwelled.

"That's Black Mountain," Frank said. "A few miles south of

our ranch. Grizzly bear country." I felt my wrist where Father's bracelet should have been.

When we arrived at the village of Howbert on the Platte River that afternoon, McCantses' foreman, Jake Ratcliffe, was waiting with horses and a box wagon. I wanted to be home again until I saw the Gray Hair with the boy at his side. The boy stared at me, as did others. I did not like this boy, and I promised myself I would watch for that one.

I saw that Ratcliffe knew Gray Hair and the boy, for he went to where they were standing and shook their hands. I learned later from Frank that the hairface worked for a mining company and also owned a ranch in the park. When I saw him on the train I knew our paths would cross again, but I did not know it would be so soon. We loaded our bags in the wagon and headed to Frank's ranch near Black Mountain.

We arrived in time for the fall roundup when the ranchers from the area joined to find their cattle after letting them roam free all summer. Now they were being rounded up the way the blue coats herded my people to the reservation. Each new calf born during the time of Leaves Coming had to be marked with its owner's brand using a burning iron from a fire. The way of the Maricats was to put their brand on all things. I was glad they had not branded my people or me.

There were two white women among the ranchers. They owned a ranch along the river. They dressed as men and rode a horse as well as any man. One of them chewed tobacco. They were friendly to me one morning when I cut my finger. The woman who chewed tobacco spit the juice on the cut and wrapped it for me. I wondered what Grandfather would have thought about these women.

I wanted to ride with the cowboys but was put to work with an old black cook named Charlie Starbuck. He'd fought in the white man's war and afterwards came west with Jake Ratcliffe to work on the McCantses' ranch. I had never known a black man. He reminded me of Grandfather. He was gentle and treated me well. I liked him. He let me tie Badger beneath the wagon in shade after Badger chased the cattle.

I did not like the work—peeling potatoes, washing dishes, and such. It was a woman's work. I was glad Grandfather could not see me now. Women rode with cowboys and men cooked. I thought The Maricats were strange.

I did not like Jake, Frank's foreman. I do not think he liked Indians. I learned there were others in the outfit that did not like me or my people, or even Charlie. Gray Hair and his son, Leonard, joined the roundup one morning, but I did not know the father at first for he had shaved off all the hair from his face. Many Maricats do this, I learned. I soon saw his eyes were still as cold as when I first saw him in Craven's office that day. Shaving would not save him from my revenge.

Charlie and I followed the cowboys in the horse-drawn chuck wagon. We cooked meals for the riders during the day. When there was time, Charlie told me stories of the war, and how his folks had been taken in chains from their homes across the great ocean and herded to this land by some of the Maricats. I wasn't surprised. I wanted to know about the mountain. Charlie told me stories about it, of bears and lions and evil spirits. He told me of a Cheyenne Indian named Bear Killer whose son, a boy about my age, was carried away by a grizzly. It was long before the whites came to live in South Park. "Some say the father's ghost still roams the valleys and forests on the mountain a'lookin' for his boy. 'Course you and me knows different," the cook said, "but them others swears it's the gospel truth. They don't know no better."

"I want to go there one day," I said.

"Just don't never go there alone, Tomas."

On an afternoon while Charlie was napping and I was peeling

apples, Gray Hair's son rode up. He yelled, "Hey, squaw. Get me a drink of hot coffee," banging a tin cup on the saddle horn. I did not look up. My blood ran from my toes to my face. The coffee was in a pot over a smoldering fire. "You hear me, boy?"

"I am no squaw," I said, squinting as I stared at him, gripping my peeling knife in my fist.

The noise woke Charlie. "What you all fussing about, Leonard Bradford?"

"I ain't fussing none, Charlie, just asked the Injun to get me a cup of coffee."

"You gets your own coffee, Leonard Bradford, and if you is wanting apple pie this evening with your dinner, you best leave this boy alone. And don't be talking smart alecky again. You hear me?" The boy got down from his horse and poured his own coffee. He looked at both Charlie and me in a hard way. I did not flinch. As he rode off, I knew this wasn't over.

It was the beginning between Leonard and me.

A few days later, Frank had me quit Charlie for the day to help move a small herd down a slope to a holding pen. I was glad. Dust was thicker than Charlie's barbecue sauce. I lost track of Frank when the animals pushed through an aspen grove. Found myself alone. A rider came from the trees behind me, and a lariat was thrown over my shoulders. Like one of the calves, I was dragged off my horse to the ground. I rolled over and saw it was Leonard. I fought free of the rope just as he was about to drag me. There were sounds of a rider coming, and Leonard drew his rope in and disappeared in the trees. Frank came around to where I lay.

"What you doing on the ground, Tomas? Horse throw you?"

"Hit a low branch," I said. I tried not to limp as I mounted again. "I'll be all right."

"We get home tonight, you rub some liniment on the sore

places," he said. "Make it better."

On the way home I thought about Bear Killer. I knew then what I would do. That night after dinner, I went into my room and got the leather parfleche out from under my bed. I took out my eagle feather and my father's lance and bow and arrows. I was able to hide them beneath my slicker. It would be dark enough when we left in the morning so Frank would not notice anything. I was not going to hurt this Leonard.

During the day, I wrapped a piece of charcoal from the fire and hid it in a pocket. I picked up wet red clay from a water hole and put it in a small tin can. Later, after lunch, Charlie let me take my horse and work with the cowboys in the afternoon. Like Hawk, I watched Leonard until I saw him heading into the trees alone—probably to relieve himself. I circled back a ways and tied my horse in the trees, then put my eagle feather on. I had to hurry. I painted my face red with the clay then drew black lines on my cheeks with the charcoal. I slipped without a sound to where Leonard was standing, pulling his pants and chaps back up. Half-hidden in brush, I screamed the loudest war cry I could. Leonard turned, and holding his pants in one hand stared like a scared doe at my painted face and the feathered lance I waved at him. He tried to run, fell, then stood to run again, hobbling like a wounded jackrabbit with a coyote snapping at his back end. I laughed out loud. I know he heard me.

I believe Leonard knew afterward it was me, but he never said so to anybody. He did tell a few of his cowhand friends he'd maybe seen the giant black-lined, bloody-faced ghost of the old Cheyenne, Bear Killer, and was barely able to escape with his life.

Later that night, Frank asked me at dinner if I'd heard about Charlie's Bear Killer.

"No" I said. "I have never heard of this Bear Killer."

Frank grinned as Grandfather might have. "Maybe you'd better get rid of those weapons you have under your bed, Tomas."

I could not get rid of my father's bow and lance, Charlie let me keep them hidden in the chuck wagon. Near the end of the roundup, Charlie, some others, and I rode one more time up the lower slopes of the mountain looking for a stray or two. "You best take these weapons with you, Tomas, 'case you run into old Bear Killer," Charlie said. He chuckled. "They's caves up there, too, 'n' you can maybe hide 'em away so Mr. McCants don't see 'em, or for a time you want to go hunting something."

On the mountain, I left the others and was able to follow a game trail along a narrow ledge and found a small cave on the edge of a cliff. I hid the bow and arrows and the lance inside the cave. I could easily get them when I needed to. I would need them, for I would be "hunting something." Soon.

CHAPTER 13

September 26, 1880
McCants Ranch
South Park, Colorado

Utu-tatapi. The time of Everything Gets Yellow.

The blue irises were gone from the meadows along the creek and irrigation ditches. Few leaves clung to the aspen trees. Hay from the meadows had been cut and stacked like the brown loaves of wheat bread baked in Libby McCantses' cookstove. The fall roundup was over. The bawling herd of McCants cattle along with those from neighboring ranches were gathered, counted by brand, and delivered to the railhead at Howbert and then hauled to Colorado Springs. I was still lonesome, but there was time to rest. It was good.

On a chilly night after dinner, I sat astride the corral fence outside and, remembering my people, stared up at the stars. I wanted to sit with my parents and grandfather and my friends around a fire and visit with them. The sound of wild geese overhead made my loneliness greater. As they passed over, a strange quiet suddenly surrounded the ranch. Even Old Coyote's howling was absent. I felt uneasy.

The moon poured a cold white light down over the land and buildings. Screaming ghosts from the moonlit night of the killings by the hairface returned. Then I knew I was hearing real screams, distant, from the emigrants' camp down along the river. Something had roused the party of prospectors there. I shuddered at the sounds, then heard the doors on the large barn slamming shut and Frank McCantses' familiar footsteps approaching.

"Something's going on out there." He stood behind me.

"Yes."

"I'm going after my rifle. Jake rode down to see. You want to come in the house?"

"I'll be all right."

"Sure?"

"Yes."

"Be right back." Frank vanished in shadows, and I heard the back door of the ranch house close. Warm light shone out the kitchen windows. Pine smoke from Libby's cookstove hung on the night air. Maybe I should have gone in.

My body went rigid and I gripped the rail as the corral fence was smashed suddenly and wild screams filled the dark. Afterward I thought I might have smelled the grizzly bear before I saw it push through the broken fence to reach for the carcass of the antelope Jake Ratcliffe had hung from the gate post earlier that day.

The bear, downwind, did not seem to see me. I sat still as the huge animal stood suddenly, and in the moonlight swiped at the carcass with a great forepaw ripping it to the ground.

"Tomas!" The back door of the ranch house was thrown open and Frank McCants, rifle in hand was framed in its light. "Tomas!" he shouted again.

I jumped as the roar of Frank's gun sounded. A window in the barn shattered. The bear grabbed the antelope in its jaws, dragging it into the shadows. Even in the darkness I could see that it favored a forepaw as it ran from the corral. I dropped from the fence rail and went to where I could see across the moonlit prairie toward the river. I saw the round form of the grizzly as it paused to stand, looking back again before it continued on to the river. There was something familiar in its limp.

McCants came to my side. "Who are you waving at?"

"No one."

"Thank God you're all right. You see which way it went?" He was breathing hard.

"No. Too dark."

McCants's foreman, Jake Ratcliffe, rode into the yard, and I went to take the reins from his horse. Like I said, I did not like Ratcliffe, and I was sure he did not like the Utes. He was younger than Frank, had red hair, and came from far across the great waters in a boat. He was a soldier in the white man's war, and when he and Frank drank whiskey, Frank called him "Sarge," and he called Frank "Captain," and they laughed about their times together before they came here to the park and the ranch. I put the horse away, returning to hear the two men.

"You talk to 'em?" Frank asked.

"Yeah. Party of ten or twelve, mostly men—couple of women and two or three kids. Heading for Leadville. Come up from Cañon City through High Park and camped down there where the river cuts through them scrub pine." Ratcliffe coughed and lit a cigarette. "They was plenty scared, Frank." Jake laughed. "Said it was big as a elephant. Come right into their midst, walking like a giant. Didn't hurt no one, just stood there and looked at 'em. You shoulda seen their faces—was a grizzly, for sure, Frank." I followed the two men into the house with its warm kitchen smells. Libby poured coffee for us. "Old three toes for sure. Could see his print in the mud. Size of a meat platter. Bold as you please. Looked like he headed back here along the river toward the ranch."

"He was here," Frank said. "Busted through the fence after your antelope. Better not hang any more game outside. No great harm done, but I don't want him to think he can drop in here when he wants to."

"Ranch work is mostly caught up, Frank. Me and Charlie and the Indian kid could go after him. Make sure he don't hurt no one." Jake forked pie into his mouth.

Frank glanced at me and then turned to Libby. I did not want to hunt the bear with Ratcliffe. I knew men like Jake. The foreman boasted of the animals he'd killed. I didn't want this bear harmed, for it was my brother. It was even possible my father's spirit lived within this bear. Was I not The Boy Who Sleeps with Bears?

"If you want to take a few days and see if you can track him down, might be all right. Probably heading up toward Tallahassee Creek or Black Mountain. It's about time for him to hibernate. Starbuck can go with you."

"We can leave first thing in the morning, Frank." The foreman turned to me. "I hear you're a good tracker, Tomas." It was wrong to kill this bear, for Grandfather said he has great medicine. "Whole Park's better off every time we kill one." Jake said. I was sure Libby saw the anger in my eyes as she stepped between us. I was silent.

"Smell of snow in the air these nights, so don't stay too long or get yourself in a tight spot," Frank said.

"Right, Frank. Fall storms in the Park ain't nothing to fool with." Jake stood and drained his mug, smiling at me in a strange way. "Got to get things together if we're leaving early. See you in the morning, Tom. 'Night, Frank—Libby." The foreman went out the back door to the bunkhouse. I would do as Frank asked.

"It will be good for the two of you to be together—get to know one another. Jake's a good man, Tomas."

"He does not like me."

"He just doesn't know you yet."

Libby placed her hand on my shoulder. "It's late. We'd best be going to bed, especially you hunters."

I went to my room off the kitchen—an old storeroom that Frank and Libby fixed for me. I heard Frank scoop coal into the stove—heard him banging the poker as he stirred the coals. He would be banking the fire for the night, just as Grandfather did in our carniva when the leaves turned—before the snows came. Libby had lighted the kerosene lamp by my bed. In the yellow light, the objects in the room seemed unreal to me. I undressed, pulled back the heavy quilt, and climbed into bed. I thought about Grandfather, my people—how it had been to live with them. As I leaned forward to blow out the lamp, I looked out into the night again. Moonlight lay like a great body of water upon the prairie. I believed the old man was out there somewhere. He had tried to come to me tonight. As I lay back down again, I threw one arm across my face. Kwiakati would be safe. I must see to it.

CHAPTER 14

September 27, 1880
McCants Ranch
South Park, Colorado

We left the ranch as the sun rose. Jake Ratcliffe, Charlie, and I were trailing alongside the Platte River where the bear's tracks could be seen in the soft mud. Smoke from the immigrants' upriver campfires was visible against the dawn sky. Jake was the first to speak. "Them tenderfeet won't stay there long after having a grizzly for their dinner guest last night."

"Bet on that," Charlie yawned as he spoke.

"Hope we don't disturb your beauty sleep none, Charlie," Jake said.

Starbuck grinned back, his eyes half-closed. He winked at me. "There's some so ugly, sleep won't help 'em at all. Ain't that right, Tomas?" I liked the old cowboy. Charlie continued. "It's like I told you last night, Jake, I didn't sign on to hunt no damn bear. Specially a grizz. When spring comes, I'm through with cowboying. Goin' somewheres warm all year and just sit."

"You stay close to me, Charlie, and I'll protect you from that critter," Jake told him.

Our ride took us past the sloughs that bordered the hay meadows south of the ranch. Vapors rose from the water's surface, and I heard wild ducks talking softly among the tall water reeds. Jake slowed his bay and slid his rifle from the scabbard. He pointed the gun in the direction of the marsh and fired it. Ducks and woodcocks exploded into the skies, followed by a single large crane struggling to rise from the cattails, abandoned by the swifter birds.

"Wait, Jake." Starbuck spoke as the foreman raised his rifle again.

I wheeled my roan mount around to see Jake fire the gun at the crane, hanging stark against the dawn. The wings of the bird were stopped in their movement as its body crashed into the slough. I kicked my horse in the sides harder than I should have. The animal lunged ahead. Charlie was quiet.

Jake caught up with me. "Spook your horse, boy?" I would not answer. "That one ain't used to guns. Should've told you," the foreman said.

"It was not the gun."

"Yeah?"

"You have killed the long legs."

"I did kill him, didn't I?" He had not heard me.

I stared down at the three-toed paw print on the ground.

"Didn't you never kill nothing, Tomas?" Jake asked.

"Go easy, Jake," Starbuck spoke. "Indians got ways different from you and me."

"I have hunted with my father and grandfather many times to eat," I told him.

"Hunting ain't always just for eating," Ratcliffe laughed. "Lord made animals and birds for man to hunt. Been hunting since I was younger 'n you, boy." I spurred my horse again, eyes fixed on the trail, though not seeing through my anger. I was not a boy, and animals and birds were part of my family.

We rode south toward rolling hills and the dark form of Black

Mountain. As clouds passed over the sun's face we lost, then found the bear's trail again. I could easily follow the animal's tracks—his way clearly marked. Taller grasses along the trail were crushed where the bear rolled about.

Charlie sniffed the air. "Snow's coming, sure."

"Little snow won't hurt us none. Fact is, it might make it easier to track," Jake added.

To the west, gray clouds were caught against Buffalo Peaks. When we reached a pond at the base of the mountain, we dismounted and let the animals graze. We sat on a turned-over wagon box alongside the water. The sun was now hidden by increasing cloud cover, yet still warm on our backs. We ate cold beans and beef sandwiches before riding on.

Soon, the jagged outcroppings of granite that formed the northwest face of Black Mountain were clear. Most of its huge hulk was heavy with dense growth of pine and juniper, barren aspens and bush. As drops of moisture blew against my face, I buttoned up my slicker. "Rain," I said.

"Thought you forgot how to talk, kid." Jake said. He rolled a cigarette, then lit it. "We'll have that bear and be sound asleep in our bedrolls before it snows, believe me."

"Never did like that darned mountain," Starbuck said. "It's right spooky. When I worked for the Stirrup Ranch, we chased a coupl'a horse thieves up the south slopes. Found one with his neck broke by a bear—other one got off."

"Anybody would steal a horse around these parts would be just dumb enough to mess with a bear," Jake said. "If a body come unexpected on a she-bear with cubs, could be big trouble."

"Why do you want to kill this bear?" I asked Jake.

"Why not?" Jake raised his head.

"This bear has not done harm," I said.

"Only a matter of time. Top of that, hurtin' someone don't have nothing to do with it. It's like I said. The bear hunts. A man hunts the bear. It's just natural. Part of God's plan."

"To hunt this bear is not good," I said. "The bear is a brother."

Jake laughed. "He ain't my brother. He may be yours. That's pure Indian talk. Way you was brought up. You'll learn better in time—man can't be a brother to a bear or any other animal. Only to another man or a woman."

"When a warrior dies, he sometimes goes into the body of a bear," I said.

"That's crazy Indian talk and I ain't going to argue with you, kid. I get my sights on that bear—he's off to the happy hunting ground for certain. You just keep us heading in the right direction and don't worry about them other things."

"Maricats." My anger would not go away. I leaned forward watching the ground, while behind me, Jake had begun to sing softly, his voice jerking to the movement of his horse. He reminded me of the Gray Hair who killed my mother. I saw the bent grass before us. "I will protect you, Brother Bear, " I whispered to myself.

The bear's path followed an old game trail that led to Black Mountain. The skies around and over the mountain had grown dark, the peak lost in a gray shroud. Snow had begun to fall. We rode through the heavy growth of forest until the only sounds were creaking leather, the horse's heavy steps, and grunting from Ratcliffe.

There were many spirits in this place. I felt them. Our horses stumbled over fallen trees as these spirits reached with gray, bony arms and fingers to hold us back. Turning, I saw the thick tangle of limbs and shrubs close behind us.

"We ought to make a camp, before snow gets us," Starbuck said.

"Plenty of time for a camp, Charlie, after we find that bear."

Ratcliffe motioned for me to push on.

We climbed higher, among the ancient forest growth where snow had begun to stick to the trees and bushes. We pushed through trees, room to silent room, crossed open grassy areas, then back into the darkness of overhead growth. We searched for a bent twig, a broken branch, or other signs from the bear's movement. Suddenly, Ratcliff pointed to where the ground was disturbed—stones, gravel mixed with the fallen snow, earth clawed aside. "It's wanting to den up somewheres," he whispered.

I saw the print of the bear's foot in the fresh earth. The paw print was huge. Chills rippled up and down my spine. Holding his rifle, Charlie moved a short distance off to the left. Jake and I dismounted, and Jake removed his rifle from its scabbard, pumped a shell into the chamber, and stepped ahead. Then, I saw Charlie's face twist as if in pain, his eyes and those of his horse open wide in terror.

A wild scream tore through the dark forest as the bear dashed from the thickets toward Charlie. I heard Charlie yell. He and his horse were thrown to the ground by the bear's great force. On the ground, Charlie struggled to free himself from beneath his horse. The bear lunged at him again, tearing with huge forelegs and claws at the old man's frail body. Ratcliffe had little time to sight and shot at the bear twice. Enraged, it swung around lunging at Jake, clawing at him, throwing his body aside. Then the animal stood snorting, grunting, and swinging its huge shaggy head and shoulders from side to side waiting for Ratcliff to move again. Then it sensed Charlie's small movement, the whimpering from his torn mouth, and it charged the cowboy again, lifting his frail body in his jaws and shaking him violently. Jake's gun was lost in the grass and weeds. He did not move from where he was thrown against a large boulder. The bear watched me. We looked at one another for a brief moment—as if we knew each other. The animal screamed again, then turned into the brush. Men hunt, bears hunt.

I sat on the wet ground, my arm around the trunk of an aspen tree. I heard the grumbling of the bear and the sounds of underbrush crushed and broken by the animal's huge body as it fled up the slopes of the mountain. An eerie silence returned, and I pulled myself up, standing weakly against the tree. As one walks in his sleep, I went to Charlie. "He is not breathing." I said. Jake pushed himself to his knees. I turned the old cowboy's body over. The top of his scalp hung down over his eyes.

Jake was crawling through the grass and snow toward us. "Charlie?" he muttered.

"He is gone," I said. "Are you bad hurt?"

"My arm and shoulder."

"There is blood upon your shirt," I said.

Jake bent down and placed his head upon Charlie's chest. "You're right. He's dead. Thanks to your Brother Bear."

The foreman's left arm hung loosely at his side. He slipped his jacket off and drew the shoulder of his ripped shirt down, flinching at the pain as he pulled bloodstained undershirt away from the torn shoulder. "My arm's broke, or least sprained," Jake said. He pulled the undershirt back up. "Help me pull this coat up, Tom. Not much we can do for my shoulder except make up a sling from one of Charlie's shirts. He sure ain't going to need it." Jake said.

I found a ragged, denim work shirt in the saddlebags. Following Jake's directions, I tore it and made a sling for his arm. I wrapped Charlie's body in his own tarp, tying the frail form over the cowboy's saddle. I wanted off the mountain.

"You'll see." Ratcliffe spoke to the old man's wrapped body.

"I'll get even with that bear, Charlie."

I looked away. I did not want to hunt the bear. Charlie did not want to hunt it. I was spared because of my power. I was not responsible for Charlie's death. What was the death of an old cowboy to me, anyway? I held Jake's horse while he mounted. It was snowing harder.

CHAPTER 15

September 28, 1880
Black Mountain
South Park, Colorado

Winds whipped the mountain. The tops of pine trees leaned away, and barren aspens bent helplessly. Screaming gusts drove the snow and ice needles against my face and into my eyes, seeping around the collar of my coat down along my back. Our horses stumbled their way to lower ground. Once there we could not tell which direction to take. Trails and landmarks were gone beneath the deepening blanket of snow. Trees and rocks were molded into mysterious shapes.

I led Charlie's horse, the old man's form stretched over the saddle, the tarp now ghostlike. I did not like being so close to the old man's body. Jake followed, slumped on his own horse hanging on with one hand, his broken arm bound up in the crude sling made from Charlie's shirt. He was drinking whiskey for the pain. I heard his voice, his words lost in the wind. "What?" I hollered back.

"We better make camp somewhere," he yelled again.

I shielded my eyes as I strained to see through the wind and snow. Already my legs and feet were wet and cold. I searched for a place to make a shelter. Through clouds of swirling snow, I led the way into a dense growth of pines where a large rock outcropping would support a lean-to. I would try to build a brush cover out of pine boughs. "This way," I shouted.

I helped Jake down from his saddle to a protected spot underneath a ledge, then tied our horses where they would have some shelter. I dragged Charlie's body to where I could not see it and returned to where Jake sat curled up beneath his bedroll.

"See if you can round up a couple of dead trees and some pine branches." The foreman's voice was weak. "There's a hatchet in my pack." He drank again from the whiskey. "That's better," he grunted.

Not far, I found many dead aspen trees knocked down long ago by snows. I was able to carry and drag several to the ledge where I leaned them against the rock. I cut boughs and wove them together, placing them over the aspen poles. I put more aspens on top of the branches so they would not blow away. With this shelter and the large pines about us we were soon protected from the blowing snow. But not from the cold.

Jake had scraped sticks and branches in a pile and made a fire. His face showed great pain as he handed me the pot. "Fill her with snow, kid." In a short time we had boiling coffee. Along with the beef and a few cookies Elizabeth had included in our lunch, we fed ourselves well. Jake drank coffee and more whiskey. We huddled down, wrapping our bedrolls around our shoulders as winds blew and snow continued to fall.

"How is your arm?" I asked him.

"Don't you worry about my arm, kid." His voice was hard, and his eyes seemed almost unfriendly. He smiled strangely.

"I have slept in the snow before," I told him. "Once in a place where we killed many deer. But, I do not like this one. It is a bad storm."

"This ain't nothing. I've seen worse," Jake said. He drank

again. "Already feeling warmer."

I had been told that when a man is about to freeze, he is sometimes tricked into thinking he is warm. Jake wanted to talk from the whiskey. I believed his hardness also came from the drinking. I saw this before when Uncle Kiko and Grandfather drank once with the soldiers at Fort Lewis. Kiko fought with his own brother-in-law. He did not drink again.

Jake looked as if he would sleep, then his head jerked up and he stared at me. Jake's tongue wobbled in the way of his words. "So you wanna paint pictures, huh?"

"I would like to," I said, surprised at his words. Snow sifted down through the boughs. I pulled my jacket up around the back of my neck as a turtle.

"Ought to put your mind to things more practical, kid, settle down. Paintin' is a white man's work or wimmin's, and 'sides, you can't eat no paintin' when winter comes and there ain't nothing in the larder. Mr. McCants won't like it none I reckon. I oughta know. When I was your age, I wanted to play the fiddle, but I had to help my daddy with the farm, then the damn war come along and I tell you, there sure weren't no time for fiddling or drawing no pictures."

I went out to gather dead grass and aspen bark for the horses. As I made my way through the blinding snow, something grabbed my pants leg. I was snagged on barbed wire from a fence. When I returned to the shelter, I told Jake of this fence.

"Could be close to Old Man Rodgers's cow camp," he said. "We was there during roundup if you ain't been too busy being a artist to remember." I remembered. "Maybe you could follow the wires to where they lead. See if you can find real shelter," Jake said.

"I do not want to be lost," I said.

"You ain't gonna get lost, kid, if you do like I say. Just hang onto the wire and don't take no chances." I could follow the fence line slow, be careful, maybe find the shack. Jake was rolling a cigarette with one hand. He coughed hard as he lit it with an ember. His eyes were half-closed from the whiskey, the cold, and the hurt from his broken arm.

"We will freeze here," I said. "You need to be inside. I will go. You keep the fire burning and try to stay awake." I brought him more wood. I held my hands over our fire one more time, then left the shelter to find the fence.

I tossed my lariat over my shoulder, leaned into the wind and snow and felt for the top wire of the fence, not knowing which direction I should go. The wrong way and I would waste my strength and go nowhere—perhaps freeze to death. I moved slowly, trudging step-by-step, following the wires one fence post at a time. The winds sucked my breath away. I clung to the wires as my body was swayed from the heavy gusts pushing and pulling me with their frigid arms. I walked until my feet burned from the cold. I came to a tall post. A gate, I thought. The wires ended and a terrifying fear gripped me as I reached out into the snow. I called desperately into the screaming cold and the deadly emptiness of the storm.

I would have to return to the small shelter, where I knew we might freeze when night came, or move from this post into the storm to search for shelter that may not be there. A cow-camp shack. I tied my lariat to the post and, making sure it would not come loose, stepped into the blinding fury of the blizzard holding out one arm, groping as old blind Pazio had moved about through our camp on the reservation.

I tripped, dropping the rope and hitting my knee against what felt like a feed trough. I grabbed at the snow with my hands scooping up the rope and made myself stand. Then, in the swirl of snow I saw the shape of a shack almost in front of me. I tied the rope end tight to a rail and pushed the door open. Inside it was cold but it would offer shelter. There was an iron stove and dry wood in one corner—a box of matches and candle on a small table. There were bunk beds with bedding. In a pine cabinet I found canned goods and a jar of coffee.

The wind and snow whistled through a break in one window. I pushed rags through the hole. I removed my coat and gloves. I built a fire to warm my hands and body. I would not return for Jake. What was a white man to me? A man who hunted only to kill. Let him freeze to death for his ways, just as hairface would pay for his. It was good.

I put my coat, hat, and gloves on. I could not let him die. As I went out into the storm again, I followed the rope to the wire fence. Back at the shelter, I found Jake bent over asleep. I shook him awake.

"I have found the cabin," I told him.

"Leave me be. I want to sleep," he muttered. "Leave me be."

"No. Wake up. We must get to the small house or you will freeze." I shook him again. He tried to slap me.

I got our horses and was able to make Jake stand. I led him to his horse where I pushed and shoved him into the saddle. We followed the fence line to the shack, and after helping him down, I walked him and dragged him inside to one of the beds. By now the cabin was warmer. I returned to get Charlie's body and his horse. I put the horses in an old shed outside. I left Charlie's body there also.

I was not ready for what happened next. As I pushed the door of the shack open, Jake stepped out from behind it, wild-eyed and holding the hatchet and screaming. He swung it at my head. I dropped to the floor.

"Damn Indians!" the foreman screamed. "You ain't gettin' me. I'll kill you all first!" He waved the hatchet about. He was out of his head—maybe from pain or whiskey. Probably both.

I had seen this before in a man whose foot became swollen and poisoned when he stepped into a bear trap. A soldier had given him wine to drink. "They're out there. All over the place. Damn it." He held the ax out as he staggered toward me again.

I stepped aside, then grabbed his arm, pushing him down. His head hit the corner of the iron cook stove and he fell to the floor, suddenly still. I dragged him to the bunk and, retrieving the lariat from outside, tied him down, wrapping his arm in the sling again. I banked the fire and made myself a place to sleep close to the stove. Jake was snoring. He was still alive.

In the morning the winds were still, the skies clear. A bright sun rose to cold blue prairies. I built a new fire and made coffee. I heard Jake complaining. "What happened here?" he asked. "What's this?"

I turned to see him tugging at the ropes around his body and bunk. "Too much whiskey, I think—and the pain in your arm. I was afraid you would hurt yourself." I did not want to tell him all the truth. "Are you all right?"

"Feel like I been run over by a herd of buffalo. You can have my breakfast, if there's any. I won't never eat again."

I untied him, found a can of soup, and made him eat some. I ate the rest of our beef. After we were warmed up, we struck out for home, hiding our eyes from the blinding sunlight. It was Charlie's last ride.

CHAPTER 16

October 1, 1880
Fairplay, Colorado

They came on foot, in wagons, in buggies, and on horseback to the mining town called Fairplay and the white church. I heard in their talk anger and fear for the bear's killing of the old cowboy. Among the faces was one belonging to a man I felt I had known another time in another place. This man stood inside the door taking the hands of all who went into the church. He did not take mine. He reached toward me then dropped his hand. He spoke. "Well, well. I believe it is Tomas, Tomas—whatever. What are you doing off the reservation? Have you run away?" He stared straight into my eyes, grinning as does the wolf at the small rabbit he has cornered. "Must I call the soldiers?" It was the agent Jabez Craven.

I shoved past him, bumping into Alex Comstock at Frank's side. "Easy there, Tomas, there's plenty of room," Alex said.

Craven's green glasses and hat were gone. He was dressed in black. His brown hair was cut and combed, but his voice was the same as the one I'd heard on the morning he had given Pagits and me the paper to hunt. I tried to hide in front of Alex, and behind Frank and Elizabeth.

A woman began to make music from the organ. All had come to hear again of Charlie Starbuck's dying. It was a strange way of the whites and not good for me. I felt many eyes upon me as we went to one of the benches in the church. There was talk around us of going after the bear. I wanted to tell them it was not Brother Bear's fault. We had followed the trail to his mountain the day that Charlie was killed. Some said Colonel Bradford was offering money to anyone could kill the bear.

"How could Charlie have known all these people?" Elizabeth whispered.

"They're not Charlie's friends, Libby—just want out of the house. Maybe came to hear Reverend Craven, the new preacher."

"Jabez Cravens got the wild fire of an evangelist about him," Alex said.

I watched the agent, now called a minister, as he greeted people at the door.

"Some say he acquired a reputation among the ranchers and miners around Gunnison for his sermons supporting western expansion at all costs," Alex said. He grinned at Frank.

"I've heard he has a fondness for the communion wine," Frank said.

"Hush," Libby scolded the two men. "This is a funeral."

I stared straight ahead, watching this Craven. He went to the front of the church to stand with his arm and hand on the pine box with the old man's body inside. I did not know how he could do this. He held the God-book in the other hand and began speaking.

"Friends, I welcome you today and say to you that I am pleased to serve the Fairplay community as your new minister. I'm glad to see so many of Charlie's friends here, too. We're gathered to mourn the passing of one of our own, Charles Anton Starbuck, known by most folks hereabouts as 'Charlie.' He worked for Frank and Elizabeth McCants." Craven turned as if to look at Frank and Libby, but he looked straight at me. I squirmed in my seat.

"Text for my sermon today is taken from First Kings verse thirty-four. 'And David said to Saul: Thy servant kept his father's sheep, and there came a lion, or a bear, and took a ram out of the midst of the flock, and I pursued after them, and struck them, and delivered it out of their mouth.'"

He shouted, reminding me of Grandfather's friend Azumpitz. I did not know the meaning of most of his words, but I felt his anger. My heart hopped in my chest and I jumped straight up as the man slammed the book on Charlie's box. He moved back and forth as a lion that is caged.

"'And they rose up against me, and I caught them by the throat, and I strangled and killed them.'" He shouted now as in a war dance, reaching out and strangling a spirit I could not see.

"Lots you folks probably wondering what Philistines got to do with a fellow like Charlie Starbuck. Well, my friends, Charlie Starbuck went up on Black Mountain to do battle with one of them Philistines and was brought back in a buckboard last week torn up terrible. Deader 'n a doornail."

He smacked Charlie's box again.

"There ain't nothing new about Philistines. Philistines been a plague to good folk like you and me since the beginning of time. Bible's full of stories about 'em. They're like sores on a mare's rump, burrs under a saddle. Folks coming west found 'em around every bend: bandits, Kiowa, Arapaho, Ute, Commanch', and Cheyenne, specially them Cheyenne—kind we put to rest at Sand Creek." The preacher held his bowed head in one hand "Rest their savage souls."

"Amen!" some folks called out.

He was speaking to me. I was sure he knew of my power to

stay alive even though I'd lost the bracelet. I was frightened once by Azumpitz when he came to cure my father of a pain in his belly. I wanted to hide again.

Frank put his hand on my shoulder. "You all right, Tomas?"

"Yes."

Craven went on. "Well, I'm telling you we been needing another David today—man from our own midst—to confront the dreaded demon that stalks the caves and lonely valleys of that dark domain called Black Mountain."

There were shouts and hands clapping from people sitting near.

"And that man's here with us this morning, friends." The minister's voice shook. "Right over there by the window." The congregation clapped, some shouting again. "Colonel C. W. Bradford."

"This is absurd," Libby muttered.

"He's got a style of his own, that's certain," Alex said.

Frank was shaking his head. It seemed to me he was trying not to grin.

"Colonel Bradford and a few others spoke to me before the service. They've generously offered a thousand dollars to whoever slays this giant," Craven said.

More people shouted and clapped their hands.

The minister leaned against Charlie's box. "Thank you, brothers and sisters. I'm told there'll be a meeting over to the Brass Rail right after services to organize a hunt. "Now, my friends, let's close this service for our friend Charlie Starbuck by singing number one hundred twenty-three in the hymn book." The people began to sing.

I could not see when all stood, but the hair on the back of my neck rose up. Sounds from Bradford's direction were the same

I'd heard that moonlit night of the killings. They cut across the room like cold winds. It was the voice of the man with the gray beard like the web of the spider. The man who sang the God song while his riders tore our tents down, trampled and murdered my mother, my aunt, my cousin Pagits, and others.

The force of my own anger suddenly drove out my fear. As the sound of the man's singing went on to fill the small church, I knew the promise made to me by the grizzly of my vision would soon come true.

CHAPTER 17

October 8, 1880
Howbert
South Park, Colorado

A warm sun melted most of the snow that had fallen. Then, rain fell for several days, wrapping the ranch, its residents, and guests in a cold, wet blanket. On the morning of the hunt, members of the hunting party awakened to clearing skies. Damp clothing had to be hung to dry in front of stoves and fireplaces. I was given the task of building and lighting fires in the main ranch house and outbuildings. The wood sticks Frank gave me to light the fires made it an easy job. Other hunters began to arrive, and Libby served them breakfast and coffee. I was eager to accompany the hunters. I asked Frank once again. He stared at me, and then smiled.

"You sure are hell-bent, aren't you, boy?" His voice became serious. "You can go, but if we happen on that bear, don't try anything foolish. Right or wrong, you can't risk your life trying to save an animal. You are living in a new world now. Understand?"

"Yes," I said. He did not need to remind me.

My mind was on Bradford and my plans for him. Following breakfast, we mounted our horses. Hannibal Perry, an old fur trapper and South Park rancher was picked to head the hunt.

When we had mounted our horses he counted us. "They's thirty-four of us, including four boys and three wimmins. That ain't countin' seven dogs. Near as many bodies 'n' animals as rode Bull Run." There was nervous laughter.

Perry shrugged his head in the direction of Black Mountain, its top still shrouded in mist. "Let's all 'member, folks. This ain't no turkey shoot. That bear's been shot least twice and its madder 'n hell. Any one of you runnin' into the damn thing, fire your weapon three times. If you others can get there, go. When it's over or if sundown's comin' and we ain't killed it, we'll rendezvous down at them beaver ponds, foot of chimney rock, and we'll take another body count. Won't be able to find anybody up there after dark anyways, so don't get lost. And watch them high places. That rain's made the ground soft. Person could fall that quick."

"I can tell you right now, Perry, me and my boys aren't coming home till that devil's dead." It was Bradford. He'd looked my way as he spoke. I did not like his voice. His son Leonard was next to him.

"Anyone else?" Perry waited.

"I lost a yearling to that bear last month, Perry. Just want to say up front, I'm kicking in another hundred in gold for whoever kills the damn thing." Tom Hardin, boss of the Lone Tree outfit tossed a small leather pouch to Perry. Reverend Craven coughed. "Oh yeah, 'fore we get to going, Reverend Craven wants to say a few words," Perry announced.

Craven reined his horse about. The minister removed his hat and raised his face to the skies. "Oh, God," He shouted at the autumn morning, pausing as if waiting for some sign. He repeated himself. "Oh, God," Craven's voice fluttered, "let us each one remember the words of your great and obedient servant, David, as he went forth to fight the giant Goliath: 'They rose up against me and I caught them by the throat, and strangled and killed them.'" Craven paused.

"Amen to that," Agnes McDonnell muttered.

A horse snorted. Another horse farted. A man laughed nervously. The minister continued. "When we, your servants, return home today from this divine quest, may we assure this here community, as David did Saul, that we may not have killed no lion but we sure got us a big mean grizzly bear." Craven waited again, glancing out at the bowed heads of eager riders. "Amen."

"Let's ride," Perry yelled.

There was loud cheering as we moved slowly, a single force, away from the ranch. The hunters laughed and shouted to one another as their horses began to trot, then gallop slow, pounding the wet earth like the beating of war drums.

I gripped the reins of my horse and as we gained speed, I felt my father, Grandfather Cloud Whiskers, and the others—Pagits, Topotsuk, Quinch—riding at my side, painted for battle, our lances held proudly, their feathered tips sweeping in the wind. It was this way with The People when we rode into battle. In the distance, the remaining leaves on the aspens and oaks on the slopes of Black Mountain were becoming visible—dabs of yellow, red, and orange war paint. "It will be a good day to die," I told myself, although a part of me did not believe this.

A wave of riders and yelping dogs washed against the slopes of the mountain. They were a river gone wild, thundering up dry streambeds, dashing along old game trails. They were separated from one another, and then came together like the sticks and branches that are carried by angry waters.

The horses slipped, sliding on loose rock and soaked earth. The riders complained and swore to one another, adding to the noise and confusion of the climb. We began the steeper rise through deep grass and dried bushes toward the plain of a low mesa that was the first step to the mountain's summits. To the lodge of Kwiakati.

The hunters found the bear's trail marked by blood and bent, broken grass. From the top of the mesa, riders hollered to those below. Frank and Alex were somewhere ahead. I lost track of Bradford, but I would find him. First I must find the ledge leading to the cave where I'd hidden the bundle with my father's weapons.

I drew back on the reins of my horse, falling behind the hunters. I turned toward the far side of the mesa and the granite cliffs. Somewhere behind me I heard the snorting of a horse, the sound of breaking branches, then silence. A lagging hunter. Because of the heavy rains, chunks of the ledge leading to the hiding place were washed away and I was forced to tie my horse to a tree and make my way on foot—as a squirrel in a place where the trail was almost gone.

I must have my weapons.

My heart beat wildly as more rocks gave way beneath my feet and I had to clutch a large root growing out of the rock. More gravel and stone fell to the boulders below. The root held and I was able to pull myself along.

Water dripped from the ceiling of the cave, running down the walls to form pools on the floor. Mud and stones lay about. In my excitement to unwrap the rawhide bundle, I paid little attention to the sounds of more falling rocks outside the cave. The bundle was damp and covered with green. I opened it shakily and held the bow and arrows, trembling at what I must do. With my fingers, I wiped the red mud from the floor of the cave and painted war streaks upon my face with it. I picked up Father's lance as well and went outside again, asking Kwiakati for success in my revenge. I saw Grandfather's form in the churning clouds overhead and heard his words again: *"There can be no more wars, Tomas. One must find new paths to bravery."*

"I have found that new path, Grandfather," I muttered. "I am going to use my father's bow to drive an arrow through the heart of the man who murdered my mother."

I was not going anywhere. Turning, I saw that much of the ledge leading back to my horse was gone. It lay below me—a pile of stones. I kneeled, peering down as my mind and body filled with anger. The ground above the ledge was beyond my reach. I was trapped.

I was startled again by sounds of brush breaking and the clack of hooves on rock, now below where much of my ledge lay. I did not move. I did not believe it was the bear—only a hunter, apart from the others. In the distance, I heard the sounds of barking dogs. I was about to call out, then held my breath as Colonel Bradford stepped out from the trees leading his horse, his rifle held in the other hand. He paused to kick at the rocks and dirt that had fallen. He picked up a rock, held it in his hand, and studied it. Far out across South Park I saw Frank and Elizabeth McCantses' spread. The Platte River lay upon the land like the silver chain of the peace medal. Shafts of sunlight shot through the clouds. After I'd killed Bradford, I would flee. No matter, I told myself. The Gods delivered Bradford to me. He was within range of the arrow I had chosen for him. He stalked me. I had not only eluded him but now had him in sight.

I removed the iron-tipped arrow from the old quiver and placed it against the rawhide bowstring. I drew it back slowly, my eyes on my quarry, sure as that day I killed the elk in the snow. Bradford paused to light his pipe. The man would not live to taste its smoke. I remembered his eyes—when I had gone with Pagits to see Craven—cold and gray as the mists that even now hid the home of Brother Bear somewhere above the sunlight. I heard the screams of my mother again on that moonlit night. The rawhide string snapped, breaking—cutting against my wrist. Bradford turned his head at the sound. I ducked back.

He looked up, then bent to pick up more of the rock, placing it in his saddlebag. He mounted his horse and moved away, in the direction of the distant yelping of dogs. He had not seen me. The rawhide string was rotten from age and the dampness of the cave where I had hidden the bow. I could not believe it. Even my father's lance was warped and rotten. I had been too eager for my revenge to see this. I could not travel on. I could not return. I was trapped on the ledge. I sat down. I ate one of my sandwiches. I was unable to protect the bear or to have my revenge. I did not want to call out for help. I was ashamed. Fear replaced my anger.

Chilled, I remembered the fire sticks in my pocket. The bit of sunlight had dried most the branches and pinecones on the ledge before it went behind the snowcapped peaks in the west. There was also dead pine jutting out of the rock wall where I was trapped. I built a fire in the entrance to the cave as a few scattered gunshots sounded above. Still no one came. I was alone. A great Ute warrior, with weapons that were rotted—and useless. A brave Capote unable even to avenge the death of his mother. A wise man lost upon a ledge on Black Mountain. Glancing westward, I saw the slow, easy wings of Hawk, circling against the dusk.

CHAPTER 18

October 9, 1880
Black Mountain
Colorado

Darkness came. I drew my jacket tight about my neck. The night air grew damp. I crawled, gathering pinecones and scraps of wood, tossing them on my fire. As I sat in its little light, I thought how I had failed in my quest. My fear and anger grew. I was trapped on a ledge on Black Mountain. I was angry with the murderer Bradford, the agent Craven, Frank and Elizabeth, my grandfather. The bear of my vision quest that promised I would have my revenge had been a dream. The old man's Gods were dreams.

I picked up Father's bow and arrows and his lance. There was no power in them. They were rotted with age, useless in this new world. A white world, Frank said. I broke them over my knee, then tossed the pieces onto the fire. They would burn to keep me warm.

As flames licked at the faded designs on the rotted weapons, I remembered a winter day within our carniva watching father scrape arrow shafts with a bone tool to make them straight. His large rough hands moved with skill as he decorated the shafts. It was good that day to sit with him by our warming fire as rain and snow outside drummed against the hide walls of the tent. Mother sat near us, stringing the blue berries from juniper trees into a necklace, while she sang softly.

I thought of the Apache girl, Dawn, and the warm New Mexico night, perfume from wildflowers, scent of yucca soap upon her skin. I closed my eyes and heard the pounding of drums, the growl of Kwiakati at Bear Dance, the chanting dancers as they celebrated the awakening of the bears and the coming alive again of the earth.

A coyote howled somewhere. I swallowed in the dark, the lump growing in my throat as I heard Mother's soft voice and felt her strong arms, listened again to Grandfather's song that autumn day by the creek—his voice like the rattling of dry weeds. I heard Aunt Kanav call Pagits and me from the meadows at dusk as I sat, huddled alone.

My anger began to melt away. My body heaved, then retched and I cried tears again like a woman. Would I ever be a man? Afterward, I sat quiet, staring into the few coals left. The burned arrow shaft glowed red—almost gone. When a man grew older, were memories of his life all that remained the same? Did Brother Bear remember the land—this mountain as it was before the Maricats came to build their fences, a time when he knew no fear, when all living things fled before his heavy step? Brother Bear had not changed—could not change. He would die by the hands of hunters who feared him. I did not want to change, but I did not want to die.

The feathers of the ptarmigan and the fur of the rabbit turn white when snow falls so that they might survive, yet within they are the same bird and rabbit. Is it this way with a man or woman? Can one change in ways that allow him to survive yet hold on to the teaching of his fathers and grandfathers? I could not turn white. Underneath the new clothes Elizabeth had given me, I was still Tomas—Tomas Dequine, the son of Chavas, grandson of Cloud Whiskers. This I would not want to change, but could I learn to live in the white world of Frank and Elizabeth McCants? These things filled my head, whirling as leaves in the winds, and I knew that I no longer cared about Bradford or the others. My desire for revenge seemed distant. Frank was right. I could not save Brother Bear.

There was a flutter of wings, and Hawk dropped from the dark to sit by my fire. She began at once. "What is it that you want, Tomas?"

"I want to be off this ledge, to return to Grandfather to sit once more with him in front of his fire. I want to know more of his Gods. I want to hold Badger, run with him, play with him. I would like to see Uncle Kiko—even Frank and Elizabeth and Alex Comstock. I want to live. I want to become a maker of pictures."

That night I slept with many dreams. I awoke in the morning to sounds of gunfire and dogs yelping far above. I was stiff and sore, but I looked away to see clear skies. Then leather creaked from above my ledge. I raised up. Colonel Bradford sat high above upon his horse. He was grinning down at me. His slitted eyes hid the cold gray of death that I knew waited for me. I watched as he climbed down from his saddle and slowly removed his rifle from its scabbard. "Well, ain't this a stroke of good fortune." Bradford waved his rifle at me. I sat up quickly at the sight of the man standing above. It was not a good day to die. Not yet. "What in hell?" Bradford laughed. "Ought to see your face, boy. You got red mud all over it."

I touched my cheek with my fingers, not taking my eyes from the man, trying to decide if I should leap to the rocks below. Bradford kneeled down, rifle in hand. I would look him in the eyes. Then he stood again and leaned the gun against a tree. He removed a rope from his saddle, forming a loop at one end. I moved back into the mouth of the cave. He would not hang me.

"Get out here, boy," Bradford yelled. "Tie this around your waist. Folks been looking for you since daybreak. Frank's near to having a fit. Got that damn bear cornered someplace up above."

I did not believe his words, but I had no choice. I grabbed the rope, and grunting, Bradford pulled me up from my ledge to where I stumbled, kneeling on the ground. He reached out and took my hand, helping me to my feet. I stood stamping my legs awake.

"Well, ain't you going to say nothing or would you rather end another night on that ledge?"

"I would not," I said. I tried to mutter a thanks.

"Get yourself together and hop on back of my horse. We found your roan horse wandering around. Frank's got it somewheres up above."

"I will walk," I told him.

"Get up here," he said. I stepped back and turned to run, limping into the trees.

"Damn it, boy . . ." Bradford shouted after me. "Get back here."

He could not see me now among the aspens. My fear made it easier for me to move. He rode back and forth a few times, then I heard the sounds of his horse as he rode away. I kept moving. The ground grew steeper, and as I stumbled around large rock formations I saw in the distance other riders heading up the mountain. I came out from the trees and stopped suddenly. Jabez Craven sat on a log with a boot off. He was rubbing his foot. I was thankful to see him. He looked up at me and smiled. "Lord didn't mean for decent God-fearing men to wear cowboying boots like these," he grumbled. "I'm real glad to see you again, boy."

I fell to the ground, exhausted but relieved. Craven put his boot back on. He stood, looking down at me. My mouth hung open. The minister held a revolver in his hand. It was pointed at my head.

CHAPTER 19

October 9, 1880
Black Mountain
Colorado

"Hold still, boy," Craven hissed, his voice like Tukwuapi. "Still, I said. Don't move. Captain left you in my charge, and I know exactly what to do with you. Same as we did with your kind at Beaver Creek." He whipped his riding quirt across my face. My cheeks stung, my eyes watered. I heard his rattles. I did not move—tried not to breathe. He struck me again. "Stand up now, get over there." He waved the gun toward a game trail leading between large boulders into the trees. I was trembling from fear and hunger. I could not believe what was happening. My feet were frozen to the ground. He cocked the revolver. I made myself move. "Over there, boy."

I did what he said.

"No do-gooder cowboy like your friend McCants is going to find your red hide, boy—then get all over us like they did after Sand Creek. Start hiking. That way." He waved the gun again in the direction of the trail. "We'll just find us a nice quiet place away from prying eyes." His thin lips made a small grin. His tongue flicked in and out. "You're going to die boy—die from the stray bullets of some stupid, blind-eyed bear hunter. It'll be a sad, sorry accident but don't despair. I'll do your funeral."

He took a bottle from his back pocket. It was the white man's whiskey I was sure. The gun remained pointed in my direction as he pulled the cork with his teeth and drank. He tossed the empty bottle into the brush then slithered backward, gun held in one hand, groping with his other for the reins of his horse. "Killed 'em at Sand Creek like they was rats in a corncrib. Even babies." He was muttering as he found the reins and was able to climb to the saddle. "You like to sing, don't you, boy?" He looked down at me. I said nothing. "I thought all you heathens liked to dress up in your feathers and sing—play your infernal drums and scream your heads off." Craven began to sing. "Rock of ages, cleft for me . . . Sing, boy."

My guts turned to ice. It was the voice I'd heard at old Charlie's funeral—the voice I'd heard that moonlit night my mother and the others were murdered. But Craven was not scalped as that man was. His hair was thick, still the color of the fox. I did not have to sing. The minister stopped singing as shots were fired from within a large pine grove above us. The hunters were moving our way. Craven's face and thin nose remained pointed at me, but his eyes darted toward the sounds, and when he looked back to strike, it was too late.

I dove at him to drag him from his horse. He whipped his gun around drunkenly to fire. I did not believe what I saw. As he held the gun out, the arm of his coat was pulled back, and I caught sight of Father's silver bracelet wrapped around his skinny wrist. Great power flowed into my body.

"You wear my father's bracelet, old man, and you will rot in the white man's hell that you preach of. Shoot. What do I care for you and your drunken hide? I am a man," I shouted, praying to Grandfather's Gods as I moved to drag the man from his horse. He fired the gun. The shots went wild, one grazing my leg. In my fury I felt no pain. He pounded hard upon my wrist with the crop, and I felt my grip on his arm slipping. Suddenly my fingers were caught on the bracelet. I jerked furiously at him again until he dropped his gun. I dove for the revolver. Craven swung his horse around, spurring it, reining it back hard so that it rose on its hind legs to trample me. I rose to hands and knees as its hooves came down but rolled sideways to escape. The gun would not fire. It was empty. The horse reared again, but in his drunkenness, Craven fell off the rear of the animal, and it ran. Dazed, I lay on the ground, struggling to rise. Craven scrambled to his feet staggering to where he picked up a large piece of granite. He was shouting— preaching again. He was crazy in his head.

My leg was throbbing from the wound. I forced myself up on my knees, then fell facedown, barely able to roll onto my back. Craven hovered above my head ready to smash my skull with the rock. I would die, and nobody would know the truth. Suddenly the man looked away from me. His face twisted, his eyes seemed to stare at some horror. The rock was still clutched in his claw hands above my head.

The bear crashed out of the bushes to stand as a giant, towering above both of us. It screamed with wrath and the pain from its wounds. It moaned, the sounds echoing across the mountainside. It was a sound and sight even I would not want to hear again.

Craven stared at the animal, then threw the rock at it. He turned to run, stumbling and falling, with the bear now upon him, snarling ferociously. It swiped at the minister with huge forearms, the long claws tearing the man's clothing away, ripping at his face and chest. The bear picked up the man in its jaws and shook him so hard that his red hair came off his head. Hunters came from the direction of an aspen grove above us, firing again into the animal's huge body. The bear turned toward the men and horses, then looked in my direction and into my eyes before falling to the ground. Both the bear and

Craven lay still. The man's red hair lay upon the ground. The last thing I saw was the jagged scar from the long ago scalping across the top of his bare head.

I felt a cold damp rag against my forehead, and I opened my eyes, seeing the faces of Frank, Captain Bradford, and some of the other hunters. "You were near a goner, Tomas," Frank spoke to me as he wiped my face with the cloth. He lifted me carefully to a sitting position as Bradford handed me coffee and a sliced-up apple. I ate slowly. I'd been wrong about Bradford. His eyes were warm. Friendly. I'd been wrong about many things.

Hannibal Perry had cut one of my pants legs off and was just finishing bandaging the wound where Craven's bullet had grazed my flesh. Perry grinned at me. "They's justice in this old world after all, by gosh," the old trapper said. "It's a pure wonder that old grizz finished off Craven before he hurt you any worse, boy. I can't understand why it didn't go after you, too," he said. "Unless you got some inside track. We was behind you a ways, and that grizz sure had enough time to do you in, likewise."

I knew why.

I saw Craven's body covered with a tarp. His red wig lay atop his body. Justice, not revenge, I thought, hearing Perry's words and remembering the promise of the bear that came to me that night in the place of the Long Ago People. It had not promised revenge, but a thing called resolve.

When I felt stronger, I was helped on my mount and we began the slow trek down the mountain's slopes to the ranch and a place of honor in Libby McCants's kitchen, where I feasted on homemade soup and pie. Later that evening, I was treated by the doctor from Fairplay. I did not realize it as I closed my eyes that evening, but my journey into the white world was to continue.

CHAPTER 20

(Three years later)
November 12, 1883
Denver, Colorado

The streets are lighted by the glow of gaslight. Upuna maa-tukwuci, the time the leaves all fall. The whites call it November. For three winters past, this room has served as my studio and living quarters. Shortly after the death of the bear, I came to study under Alex Comstock and to attend the white school.

Cold winds have blown since dawn, throwing sand and leaves against the windows of my room. Bare tree branches claw at the glass panes, and in the wind's whining I hear the cries of Old Coyote along the deserted streets. I have been looking at a small oil painting completed when I came here. The work was hidden away then behind a chest in my room as one would hide the bodies of the dead in a crevice or cave so that their spirits cannot return to haunt the living. As I run my fingers across its surface I remind myself it is only paint and canvas. Jeanette Comstock, my tutor's wife, found the work this morning when we moved the large pine chest in my studio.

The painting contains all that I remember of the mountain, a foreboding form against gray skies, black with pine and spruce. There are splotches of leafless aspen trees standing like gray whiskers of old men, the thick stubble hiding wrinkled valleys—valleys where death waited upon its slopes that day. In these colors—raw umber, rich Prussian blue, strokes of Payne's gray, I hear again the wind, and feel the damp cold upon the mountain's lonely northwest face and the narrow ledge I was trapped on.

At times, I still hear the screaming of the bear and the wailing of the murderer Craven as he stood like the white man's Moses amid a fall of rotting twisted timber, the strange hair wig slipping crookedly on his head. He was mad—ranting and singing, almost blind to the grizzly bear lunging toward him. He faced up at empty skies bellowing the same song he'd sung on the night of the killings. He was Upu piikati—the evil shaman.

Afterward, when it was known that Craven was dead and the bear killed by the hunters, newspapermen came to South Park to ask many questions of the events as they happened. Alex Comstock made a fine drawing of the animal, showing how it stood to face Craven and the hunters. It was printed in one of the Denver newspapers.

After his death, large posters were found in Craven's home in Fairplay. In these he carried a sword and wore a large gray wig and beard. It was believed this was the same one he wore the night my mother and the others were killed. Frank told me Craven had been an actor making talk to others from the stage. My father's silver peace medal and my mother's beaded necklace were also found in the man's home in Fairplay.

There were letters to Craven from a sister in Minnesota, in which it was learned that when he was young, his father and brother were killed by the Makuta in the Dakotas. Craven had been scalped then, yet had lived because of his bad power. He had been placed in an asylum, then released to a white church and sent west as a reservation agent.

In the shadowed corner of my room tonight, there are the few possessions that were my father's. They have been returned to me. There is the silver medallion and chain, Mother's necklace, and the flute made from wood of the red cedar cut long ago from ancient trees growing in the arid lands far south of Black Mountain. And of course, the bracelet that I now wear always. It no longer slips off my arm.

Things have been good in my life. Grandfather Cloud Whiskers lives, though he no longer rides a horse. Our friend Azumpits was able to draw out the bad spirit within the old man's chest. In a few days, they will both take their first train ride as they travel here, accompanying the Apache girl, Dawn, who has agreed to become my wife. Frank and Elizabeth will also visit. It is as Grandfather said. In this life, sorrow and joy are truly companions.

I am pleased that Jeanette has found this painting of Black Mountain. In the morning I will hang it on the wall with others, so that the light from the morning sun will fall across its face.

This will please the old man, I am certain.

AFTERWORD

I thought you might like to know how The Boy Who Slept with Bears came to be written.

In 1953 as a young newspaper reporter, I read a museum pamphlet that told of a great grizzly bear that was called Old Mose by ranchers in the South Park area of Colorado. Old Mose roamed over a large area in the state, but seemed to make his home territory on the dark slopes of Black Mountain, west of Pikes Peak, near the small village of Guffy. Over time, the bear was said to have killed at least one man and a number of cattle. Efforts to hunt him down by Whart Pigg, a government biologist, along with others proved fruitless.

Old Mose was finally shot and killed in 1904 by J. W. Anthony, a hunter using a trained dog pack. It was said that the bear had never seen dogs and was so curious about their presence that he neglected to make his escape and, as a result, was killed.

The museum information told of a boy named John Douglas who lived in Guffy and who reportedly saw the bear one morning near town. One cold day in April, my wife and I drove to Guffy to see if we could find Douglas, who would have been an old man by that time, if he were still alive. We stopped at the General Store in town and inquired if Douglas still lived there. The proprietress had not heard of Douglas and suggested I speak to an elderly gentleman warming himself at a potbelly stove.

I was told I must speak loudly, as the man had a hearing defect.

"Do you know of John Douglas?" I shouted. The man's light blue eyes seemed to come more alive as he smiled.

"John was my cousin," he said. "But you never could believe John."

This was my introduction to ninety-year-old Alfred Dell, an original resident of the region, along with a host of other early settlers of the area. In the following months, I had the pleasure of meeting Alfred Dell's son, cowboy Charlie Dell; longtime ranchers Bob and Bill Witherspoon; Mrs. Witherspoon; a cousin of Whart Pigg; and other old-timers all now passed. Mrs. Witherspoon served me homemade apple pie while recounting that it was at the Teaspoon Ranch where J. W. Anthony and Whart Pigg trained dogs using a live brown bear.

When Old Mose was finally killed in 1904, the Denver Post printed a full-page spread. The grizzly was reportedly forty-five years old, although I am not certain this is accurate. However, I determined that if this were true, the animal would have been born in the late 1860s—the same era when the Ute Indians lived throughout much of the Colorado Territory.

In time I learned that the bear played a significant role in the cultural and spiritual lives of the Ute people. I soon became aware of the irony in the similarity of challenges faced by the grizzly bear, Old Mose, and a Ute Indian boy during the late 1800s. As I gathered details about the grizzly, I developed a fondness and respect for his fearless stance against the approach of civilization. And how frightening it must have been for a Ute child and his people to find their centuries-old lifestyle suddenly interrupted by a flood tide of emigrants from the East. Both the Ute people and the grizzly faced threats to their survival. It wasn't long until efforts were under way to eliminate grizzly bears and the Ute people from their traditional homelands.

The actions of Colorado governor Frederick Pitkin and

his press secretary, William Vickers, inflamed the animosity toward Indians in the 1800s. Vickers wrote a cruel editorial entitled "The Utes Must Go." Additionally, lies were printed in newspapers across Colorado reporting false "depredations" (marauding) committed by the Indians.

My story details the efforts of a Ute boy to survive in a prejudicial world controlled by a government bent on his removal—or at least on his "civilizing."

—George Douthit

AUTHOR'S NOTES

The Boy Who Slept with Bears is a work of fiction. All of the characters, including young Tomas Dequine, his mother and father, his grandfather Cloud Whiskers, and others are fictional characters. A few of the events in the story were based on authentic incidents occurring in the lives of the Ute Indians in Colorado during the late 1800s. Therefore they have been included. I have also mentioned a few historically important Ute men and women who participated in treaty talks at the time. Following is information concerning what is fact and what is fiction.

Page 120—Ute Homelands

Initially, the Ute Indians inhabited all of the land that now comprises the state of Colorado. Following the western migration of non-Indians and a series of treaties with the U.S. government, the Utes soon found themselves displaced from their traditional homelands. Some Ute bands were able to retain a small area in the southwest corner of Colorado, where the magnificent San Juan Mountains and surrounding lands sustained them. However, in 1873, gold and silver deposits were discovered in the San Juan Mountains. Miners and the Ute people living there competed for the land's resources. Eventually, the government pressured Ute leaders to give up these lands to the miners and incoming non-Indians. At one point, Ute leaders struggled with the government's concept of the new boundaries, believing that they had only sold the tops of the mountains.

Still, the Southern Ute and the Ute Mountain tribes were allowed to remain in the southwest corner of Colorado, where they reside today. The Tabeguache Ute and the White River Ute bands, however, were forcibly removed from their government-appointed lands after the Meeker tragedy in 1879.

Life on the reservation was not easy for The People. They faced inadequate game due to diminishing hunting grounds, and bitter cold winters. What rations were promised through the government treaties were often late and inadequate.

Page 11—Indian Boarding Schools

Indian boarding Federal schools were established throughout the United States by the government. Officials hoped to "civilize" Native American children so they would fit into a white society. Young children were taken from their parents and sent to these schools. Traditional clothing was removed, and the Ute children were forced to wear "uniforms" and to give up their Ute language. One such school was located near Grand Junction, not far from the Ute Reservation. Reports by reservation agents during these times indicated that many Ute parents did not agree with the government's ideals. They were reluctant to send their young children to these schools.

Page 9—Indian Agents

The Indian agent Jabez Craven is a fictional character. The majority of Indian agents assigned to Ute agencies came from church-related organizations. It was their desire to help "civilize" members of the tribe. While many agents were dedicated to helping the Ute people, there were some whose motives were questionable. Jabez Nelson Trask, a clergyman from the Unitarian Church, was one of the more memorable Indian agents. He wore a tall black beaver hat, green sunglasses, and a blue naval jacket adorned with bright brass buttons. Trask was known for walking from Denver to the Los Pinos agency near Saguache in an effort to help the U.S. government save money. Trask left his position after Ute leaders lost their faith in him. He left a large sum of government cash in a bank in Denver, neglecting to use it during his tenure as agent for the Ute Indians.

Page 30—Governor Frederick W. Pitkin

In November 1879, following the slaying of White River agent Nathan Meeker, many of Colorado's citizens panicked. Articles printed in local papers across the state made false accusations against the Ute people. Many of these stories were written by newspaper reporter William Vickers, who described the Utes as being out of control and attacking settlers. Vickers, who later became the press secretary for Governor Frederick W. Pitkin, encouraged other newspapers to follow his lead. "The Utes Must Go" soon became the cry of many Colorado citizens.

Page 24—The Murders

My account of Tomas's mother and her murder is fictional. It is based, however, on a real event occurring around 1890. A small band of Southern Ute men, women, and children had been given permission to leave the reservation in order to hunt game to feed their tribe's people. As they traveled through the area called Beaver Creek, the small band was attacked while they slept in their tents by a band of renegade men on horseback. Some of the Indians were killed and others were wounded. Even though there was an investigation, the culprits were never caught.

Page 61—Treaty Talks in Ignacio, 1880

Following the Meeker incident, Ute leaders gathered in Ignacio to discuss their future with the U.S. government. The treaty talks mentioned in this section actually took place, with many of the prominent Ute leaders mentioned in the story. It was during these talks that the famed Tabeguache Ute leader Ouray died.

Page 57—Removal of the Tabeguache Utes and the White River Utes

Because of Agent Meeker's unreasonable demands on the White River Utes, there was a great deal of anger toward him by the Indians at the White River Agency. Meeker had attempted to turn the Ute men and women into farmers. The People were forced to live in square houses rather than their customary round lodges. In addition, Meeker ordered agency employees to plow up the rich, fertile pony pastures that fed Ute horses. When the Ute people resisted, Meeker withheld food rations, and even threatened to shoot their prized ponies. As a result, Meeker and some of his agency workers were slain, and Meeker's wife and daughter, along with Mrs. Price and her children, were taken hostage by some White River Utes.

Ouray, the Tabeguache leader, eventually intervened on behalf of the White River Agency captives. Even though the women and children were released, The White River Utes and the Tabeguache Utes knew that their lives were about to change. In September 1881, General R. S. Mackenzie and his troops marched 1,451 Ute men, women, and children out of Colorado and onto the Uintah-Ouray Reservation in northeastern Utah.

Page 59—Warrior Artists

In 1875, in an effort to prevent other uprisings by tribes on the southern plains, the government seized several prominent Indian leaders and warriors from the Cheyenne, Arapaho, Kiowa, and Comanche tribes and transported them to St. Augustine, Florida. There, the Native American men were imprisoned at the ancient Spanish-built Fort Marion. Although they endured harsh conditions at the fort, Captain Richard Henry Pratt encouraged the men to draw and paint about their life and times on the plains. Eventually, the pieces of artwork were sold to tourists. A pictorial history of these Native American artists can be seen in the pages of a book entitled *The Warrior Artists.* Captain Pratt founded the Carlisle Indian School, where Native American children were assimilated into the non-Indian lifestyle. Some of the men returned home, while others remained in the East.

Page 63—Saltworks in South Park

South Park is one of three magnificent valleys in Colorado. It is surrounded by mountains and foothills, and was previously named Bayou Salado (Bay of Salt) by early trappers because of the vast salt deposits in the area. In the late 1800s, a salt recovery plant was built there. Remains of the old saltworks now sit on private property in the South Park area. Over the years, Native Americans from many tribes visited the salt deposits to obtain supplies of salt and to hunt game.

Page 63—Black Mountain

The large, dark form of Black Mountain is real. It stands sentry at the end of South Park, surrounded by many historic ranch properties. It was said to have been the home of one of Colorado's greatest and most famous grizzly bears, Old Mose. The mountain is covered by lush pine forests and aspen groves.

SOME FACTS AND A FEW UTE LEGENDS TO ENJOY

Fact: The Ute tribes roamed the Rocky Mountains of Colorado, Utah and New Mexico for hundreds if not thousands of years before the white Europeans discovered the area.

Fact: The Utes were among the first Native Americans, if not the first, to ride horses. They were introduced by the Spaniards who came to the Rocky Mountains in the 1600's. The Utes were soon using horses to hunt buffalo on the Great Plains, move their camps and to make war on their enemies: the Arapahoe, Cheyenne and Comanche (from whom the Utes stole many horses).

Fact: In wars with their enemies, the Utes scalped their victims, took their weapons and clothes. In 1779, the Utes and some Apache allies joined Juan Bautista de Anza, the governor of the Province of New Mexico who commanded a force of 800 soldiers, to fight a pitched battle against the Comanches at what is now Colorado Springs and Manitou.

Fact: The state of Utah is named for the Ute Indian tribes. El Paso County, Colorado (El Paso is Spanish for "The Pass") is named for the Ute Pass Trail; the route used by migrating Ute Indians for eons. Over time, the route became a wilderness road used by trappers, mountain men, explorers, prospectors, freight haulers and eventually the Colorado Midland Railroad. Today, US Highway 24 follows the same pathway.

Fact: Manitou Springs was sacred to the Ute's as well as a number of other tribes. They all believed that the mineral springs were where the Great Spirit Manitou lived, and that the bubbles coming up in the water were from his breathing. The waters were thought to have great healing powers and were prized as a restorative by both the Native Americans and White Europeans. The springs were also a lookout point for the advancing war parties of enemy tribes, as well as the escape and choke point of the pass.

Fact: The most well known of the Ute Chiefs was Ouray, who spoke four languages and negotiated on behalf of all the Ute Tribes with Washington, D.C. The town of Ouray, in Southwestern Colorado was named for him. Some other notable chiefs of the era were Ignacio, Blacktail Deer and Buckskin Charlie.

Fact: The seven Ute tribal groups were the Mouache, Capote, Weeminuche, Leabeguache, Parionuche, Yamparica and the Unitah. They were proud and fierce in war and peace, and gifted horsemen.

During the long cold winters, the Ute people passed the time by telling stories. Here are a couple of the best...

Legend: It was said, that the Great Spirit formed a funnel in the clouds, through which he poured earth and rocks, ice and snow, and formed first the Great Plains, and then Pikes Peak, or as the Ute's called it, "The Sun Mountain Sitting Big." Some say that Sun Mountain Sitting Big is directly under the gates of Heaven, and points the way to it.

Legend: Some grandfathers told the story of the great grizzly bear, who captured the Great Spirit Manitou's daughter and forced her to marry him. They had many children, who became the Ute Nation after the Great Spirit took his grandchildren back. To punish the grizzly, Manitou forced it to walk on four feet instead of two.

It is true, that the Ute's venerated the grizzly bear above all others and celebrate the arrival of spring by having a great feast, and performing the Bear Dance, which shows the great bear coming out of hibernation and thus announcing spring, a time of rebirth.

BIBLIOGRAPHY

Emmitt, Robert. *The Last War Trail*. Boulder, CO: University Press of Colorado, 2000.

Marsh, Charles M. *People of the Shining Mountains*. Boulder, CO: Pruett Publishing, 1982.

Mills, Enos. *The Grizzly: Our Greatest Wild Animal*. Boston: Houghton Mifflin, 1919.

Pettit, Jan. *Utes: The Mountain People*. Boulder, CO: Johnson Books, 1996.

Rockwell, Wilson. *The Utes: A Forgotten People*. Ouray, CO: Western Reflections, 1998.

Simmons, Virginia McConnell. *Bayou Salado: The Story of South Park*. Boulder, CO: Pruett Publishing, 1966.

Simmons, Virginia McConnell. *The Ute Indians*. Boulder, CO: University Press of Colorado, 2001.

Smith, Anne M. *Ethnography of the Northern Utes—Papers in Anthropology No. 17*. Santa Fe: Museum of New Mexico Press, 1974.

Smith, P. David. *Ouray: Chief of the Utes*. Ouray, CO: Wayfinder Press, 1990.

United States Department of Interior. *Annual Report of the Commissioner of Indian Affairs, 1872–1890*.

About the Type

The Boy Who Slept with Bears

The body text of this book
is set in Adobe Minion Pro.

Minion is an old style serif typeface inspired by letters used during the late Renaissance-era. It was designed in 1990 by Robert Slimbach for Adobe Systems. It has proven to be a popular and adaptive type, used for everything from Stieg Larsson's Millennium Trilogy to other languages including Arabic, Cyrillic, Hebrew, Thai, and Song (Chinese). Minion is noted for its versatility, warmth and balance, making it one of the most readable and widely-used fonts available today.

www.ingramcontent.com/pod-product-compliance
Lightning Source LLC
Chambersburg PA
CBHW020645250626
47154CB00008B/2819